THE MISSING SWAN

By Garrard Hayes

Garrard Hayes

Books by Garrard Hayes

Bourbon & Blood

The Missing Swan

The Missing Swan

By Garrard Hayes

Copyright 2016 Garrard Hayes

Book design by Cigarjuice Press

For Marty. My Mentor, Father and Hero. He was the best of the best and always enjoyed gritty crime action thrillers. He would've loved this novel.

I wish to personally thank the following people for their help in creating this book: Sandy, Devan, Max and Francine LaSala my editor for her mentoring and professional insight.

PROLOGUE

The unexpected rise and fall of my crime career was built on the bones of countless insurgents, wicked thugs, and a handful of blameless individuals that just had unfortunate timing. Did they all deserve to die? The evil ones did and they got what they deserved. We all have our regrets. Some from lost opportunities or poor choices, others from lives we couldn't save.

My regrets? Something deep inside me wishes I'd hugged my parents more before they died. Maybe if I had disobeyed some orders on the battlefield, I might have saved more brothers from enemy bullets or roadside bombs, brothers who weren't lucky enough to make it home.

I returned to the States after all that training, an expert in survival and combat, and then squandered my military ambitions by not reenlisting. All my chances of becoming an officer faded away and my patriotic dreams of becoming one of the world's elite sentinels turned into a nightmare of epic proportions. I killed informants and destroyed a corrupt investigation in sex trafficking. I lost my love, ruined my life, and fled my country, narrowly escaping New York on a container ship headed to St. Petersburg, Russia.

Now I find myself constantly looking over my shoulder, on the run from the FBI, Mexican drug cartels, and the Russian mafia. And it's all because I let my idiot cousin talk me into an interview with a local Irish kingpin. The rest? Well, let's just say the rest is history.

CHAPTER ONE

The frigid night air made it hard to breathe as I weaved my way to escape deeper into the woods. The moonlight reflected off the pristine snow, leaving me an easy target. Boots crunched from behind, gaining on me fast. I panicked, but trudged on with exhausted, rubbery legs.

A single bullet screamed through the air and I felt an excruciating spike of pain as it penetrated my thigh. I watched in horror as a splash of bright red blood exploded onto the frozen pond I delicately traversed. When I collapsed, my body shattered the thin ice and I plunged into the bone-chilling slurry.

I quickly burst upwards, frantic to catch my breath, and shaking uncontrollably as my body temperature dropped and my joints shrieked in pain. I clawed at the edges of the shattered fissure with one hand and held my machine gun in the other. Gunfire from the tree line lit up the dark forest like a strobe light. Bullets whizzed overhead and splintered nearby trees. I fired one last round before my weapon slipped away and plunged below.

Huge chunks of ice broke off with each of my frenzied attempts to escape the pond, and I desperately tried to use them as leverage, but they couldn't support my weight. My hands stopped functioning from the numbing cold and I slid under for the last time. My body spent, I couldn't fight the suffocation that overtook me. I shuddered as icy water replaced the oxygen in my lungs and I sank further towards my final resting place.

As I submerged, I looked up one last time and saw beams of moonlight and a ghostly figure of a woman. Wisps of vapor floated off her hair and dress as she extended her skeletal hand and hauled me up to her rotting skull for a final kiss before I died.

Paralyzed by fear, I screamed in silence and then screamed again, forcing the sound from my throat as I shook myself awake.

I shot out of bed like a rocket and gasped. My pillow and T-shirt were completely soaked through with sweat. For a few seconds I had no idea where I was. My only clue was a dull desk lamp on a small table in the closet-sized cabin I slept in. A slight sway and groan of heavy metal reminded me that I was still on the colossal container ship *Eilbek*, which was headed to Russia.

All I wished for was a clear conscience and a good night's sleep, but it wasn't to be. Haunting dreams tormented me nightly, but this one had been different. I knew there had to be some kind of hidden message or symbolism attached to it. Premonitions, omens, or delusions, I just didn't know.

I changed clothes and left the sanctuary of my cabin to have a smoke on the ship's deck. My steps echoed off the metal walls as I made my way down the stairs and through the darkness, lit only by dim bulbs every few feet. It gave the passage the eerily familiar appearance of a New York City subway tunnel.

I reached the main landing and felt around for the metal wheel handle that opened the ship's bulkhead hatch.

I leaned all my weight into the heavy metal door

and slowly opened the hatch. It creaked in protest and then bright morning light briefly blinded me, instantly followed by a blast of frigid sea air. I stepped out onto the deck and looked for a place to smoke. Late October was getting chilly and it was only going to get colder as I made my way to my final destination somewhere outside of Moscow. My plan, if you could call it a plan, was to hunt down Viktor and kill him.

As a member of a small Russian mafia crew that operated in Brighton Beach, Brooklyn, Viktor had led an internal war to split off his group from the bigger organization and he desperately needed money to fund it. He pretended to kidnap my girl and had beaten me severely, breaking both my legs and putting me in a coma for months. When I recovered, he attempted to extort money from me to free my girl. I delivered Viktor to my superiors, but somehow he managed to escape a torture session with most of his teeth. To my surprise, he had had help from my former business partner, Kenny Shea, a dirty thug, conman, and FBI informant. I heard that Viktor was hiding under his brother's protection in Russia. I couldn't wait to see him and settle the score.

Large snowflakes floated down from the gray sky like fluffy cotton confetti. Weightlessly they descended through the air and onto the deck. I closed my eyes and let the icy flakes land on my face. For a brief moment I felt like a child enjoying the snow for the first time. I took a deep breath and let it out slowly, hoping to relieve my stress and sadness.

A sudden gust blasted me in the face, taking me by surprise. Bitter and biting, it ripped at my cheeks and ears. I turned my back to it, pulled out a hard pack of Marlboro reds, and tried unsuccessfully to light a smoke. My hands immediately grew numb as I cupped the flame, only to have it blown out each time. My frozen thumb became raw against the lighter's spark wheel. I cupped my hands again, tighter this time, and was able to light the tip of my cigarette. It glowed bright red and I took in the familiar smoke that reminded me of home.

The door creaked open behind me and I turned to see a large figure step out. He was easily half a foot taller than me and heavier by at least a hundred pounds. The crewman was in his late thirties, with a solid wide build and a full black beard. He barked something in Russian and let out a deep throaty laugh. Then continued to stare at me, waiting for a response.

"Sorry friend, but I don't speak Russian," I said.

"Okay, no issues. You're the American everyone's been talking about," he said, with a heavy accent. He studied my face for a few seconds and narrowed his eyes.

"Yes, I'm Bill, the American. What's your name?" I asked.

"I am Yuri Medved. Means 'bear,'" he said, with a big grin.

"You look bearish. I mean, kind of like a big grizzly."

"Da, you should see my sister," he joked.

"Is she bearish too?" I asked, hoping I hadn't insulted him.

"No, not really. Yuri only make tiny joke. She's beautiful and doesn't have Yuri's beard. If you saw her you'd fall instantly in love."

The wind blew hard and burned my cigarette down to the filter. Yuri took a deep breath and watched me as I flicked the cigarette over the side. The ember trailed into the dark ocean below.

"This place is no good for smoking. Yuri has better spot. Come, I show you?" He motioned me to follow.

"I'm okay here," I said, a little unsure of what he wanted.

"Just follow Yuri. We go between containers. No wind there. We smoke good and hear each other's words," he said, and walked off around a corner.

I didn't move, wondering how safe this Yuri guy was.

After a while he came back and poked his head out.

"Come on, cowboy. Yuri won't bite. Besides, you'll freeze nuts off smoking by rail."

He seemed like a likable guy, but I still hesitated feeling that this might be a trap. Finally, I took a deep breath and followed him towards the middle of the ship. The giant stacks of metal containers created rows reminiscent of buildings that lined city streets. As I passed in between them, the wind immediately subsided.

Yuri leaned against a red container and slid to the floor. He worked a soft pack of cigarettes from his jacket and lit up.

"Where are you from in America?"

"I grew up in New York City."

I sat down across from him and lit a smoke.

"The Big Apple, right? I love that city, but trouble always finds Yuri there."

He stared off at something in the distance and went quiet, looking as though he was trying to recall something.

"Yeah, I live there, or used to. Trouble followed me too. So where are you from and what do you do on this ship?"

"I from Ukraine and I cook," he answered, proud and loud.

"Really? I would have thought you worked in the engine room."

"Well, I cook and fight. I didn't see you at breakfast, but you'll have to come for lunch. Okay, boss?"

"A fighter? Is that another joke?" I asked.

"No joke, my friend. It's the ship's entertainment. We fight and we bet for big money. You like money? Bet on me. I've been on a streak, but you know, anything could happen. There are many angry people on this ship. They've lost lots of money betting against me."

I reached into my jacket and pulled out my hard pack of cigarettes.

Yuri put his hand over mine. His giant mitt was twice the size of my hand.

"Try Russian cigarette. You might like."

He quickly pulled out his own pack. The white pack with a red circle looked like something out of a war movie from the forties.

"It's Lucky Strike from Ukraine. Much tastier than your American Marlboro."

He gave me a big grin of yellow teeth and motioned for me to take one. Not wanting to insult the huge man, I slid one of his cigarettes from the pack and twisted it into my lips. Immediately Yuri put a flame to the tip. I inhaled as the tip lit and glowed red. The harsh smoke burned my throat and I let out a few coughs.

"See, it's a good smoke. Right? Cheaper than American smokes, too."

He laughed, lit another for himself, and blew out an enormous cloud of smoke.

"It's good and it's strong."

Yuri nodded and handed me his pack.

"You take these. I have plenty."

"Thanks," I said.

"I have to get back to kitchen. Lunch is at noon. Come try my food. You might be surprised by how good it is."

"Sure."

"Later, Cowboy."

We stood and he smacked me on the back so hard that I gasped and nearly fell over. After I recovered from Yuri's love tap, I finished my cigarette and headed back to my cabin.

As I opened the bulkhead door to return to the ship's interior, another crewmember came out. I tried to let him pass, but he shoved me out of the way with a grunt and a side-glance of disdain. He never stopped to look back or say a thing. I only got a glimpse of his face, but I did notice his feral eyes and thin, downturned mouth. He was about my size with a narrow wiry frame. He oozed hate and it gave me the impression he was a dangerous man.

I entered the dark stairway and climbed the metal stairs to my cabin. When I was halfway up the first set of metal stairs, two crewmembers came racing down. They spoke loudly in Russian and I pressed myself up against the railing to let them pass. They barged past me and out the bulkhead door.

The ship creaked and swayed slightly as it cut through the Atlantic Ocean. I reached the third level and walked down the corridor to my cabin. I unlocked my door, slipped inside, and locked it behind me. A solitary desk lamp lit the small, closet-sized space. A tiny table and bed filled the room.

I reached for my book, *Shantaram* by Gregory Roberts, and sat on the bed's edge. I turned to a page I'd dog-eared, read the first paragraph, and slowly drifted back into the story.

CHAPTER TWO

At noon, I locked up my cabin and headed over to the mess hall, a brightly lit, medium-sized room with six long bench tables bolted to the floor. In the back of the room was a door to the kitchen and a serving window. You could see into the busy kitchen as the staff raced around in final preparation for lunch.

Scattered crewmen sat at tables fully set with glasses, plates, flatware, napkins, and pitchers. The fantastic aroma of borscht filled the room and immediately made my stomach rumble loudly. Reluctantly, I walked towards the back of the room and sat at a table by the bustling kitchen, where I could hear Yuri's booming voice bark out orders in Russian.

Steaming, freshly baked rolls appeared at the window and a server rushed out of the kitchen and placed rolls and butter on each table. Next to arrive was a bowl of savory beef stew. I dug my spoon into the steaming mixture of chunks of beef, cabbage, beets, and onion. Before I knew it, the bowl was empty.

I scanned the room. To my surprise, it had filled up with more than thirty crewmen who ate, laughed, and talked. Everything seemed happy and normal until I locked eyes with the guy who had shoved me aside on the deck. He glared at me with a sour expression then leaned in to say something to a crewman on his left. All the men at his table then turned their heads and stared at me with stone faces. He clearly led this group and had some kind of problem with me. He whispered to the guy sitting next to him, who then stood and headed my way.

He sat down across from me and nodded a greeting.

"You're the American?"

"Do I know you?" I asked.

His expression changed to a scowl.

"Vlad will speak to you. You come now," he said and returned to his table.

I waited and tried to figure out what these guys wanted, but I knew it couldn't be anything good. I headed over. As I approached, a couple of the crewmen got up and walked away.

"Take a seat," a seated man declared, with a slight accent. "I am Vlad from St. Petersburg and this is my ship."

I sat across from him.

"What's this about?"

"I'll ask the questions," he hissed. "Do you fight? We need more fighters."

"Not interested," I replied.

"Could be big money. You do like money? Don't you?"

Suddenly a huge fist came down on the table, sending the settings, food, and beverages crashing to the floor.

"That's enough. He's with me," Yuri shouted, inches from Vlad's face, his voice filling the room. All went silent. Yuri's eyes were set with a grim expression. His jaw muscles pulsed as he gritted his teeth.

"We are done," Yuri said. "If you or your people bother my friend again, I crush you. Got it?"

Vlad only stared blankly in response until Yuri went back to the kitchen. Then he got up without a word and left the mess hall. Things went back to normal and the crewmen returned to their banter.

I returned to my seat to find a fresh steaming portion of the borsht and hot rolls waiting for me. Yuri joined me with his own large bowl.

"Vlad is nothing but trouble. Bad guy. I wanted to make sure he knows where we stand." Yuri gave me a big smile then dug into his bowl with a spoon and began devouring the food like a starving man.

"What's his problem?" I asked.

"He's desperate to beat me and win back his money. My fights are the only ones he loses money on. No one has come close, but it's only a matter of time. You'll see tomorrow night and understand."

"How many fights do you guys usually have each night?"

"Three or four, sometimes more, but heavyweights always last."

"I'm surprised Captain Kozlov allows this," I said.

"Ha. Allows it? He's our biggest bettor."

I picked up a glass of ice water and gulped it down. Just then, two men came out of the kitchen with stained white aprons and sat down with us. The one closest to me began speaking in Russian to Yuri.

"Speak English!" Yuri barked.

"Hello, I am Robert Belinsky and this is my brother Garry. We work with Yuri in kitchen. And whatever else Yuri tells us to do."

Both men were small, with close-cut light brown hair and scruffy beards. I noticed Garry had a nasty scar that started on the edge of his mouth and ended about two inches up his cheek.

Yuri must have noticed me staring at the scar.

"Garry had a run in with Vlad and his boys a while back," Yuri explained.

"Vlad cut him?"

"No, he never does the dirty work," Robert replied.

"What happened?"

"We don't talk about it. Whoever it was, we won't see him again," Robert said, with a slight smirk.

Garry nodded.

"Yeah, Vlad's left us alone since then," he said, in

a low voice. "That cold water can be a real killer."

"Our English is pretty good from watching American movies. Yes? We love the *Die Hard* movies," Robert said, his face lit up with excitement.

"Yippie ki-yay, mudderfucker!" Garry suddenly blurted out, and then sank back into his seat, embarrassed.

"I like those movies too," I said.

"Is it really like that in America, with everyone shooting guns at each other?" Garry asked.

"Only if someone messes with you," I said, and made a pretend gun with my hand.

"Whoa, watch out, Cowboy!" Robert said.

Yuri gave him a disapproving look and then suppressed a laugh.

"Listen, friend, you need to be extra careful now that you know ship's politics. Vlad has a way of making things difficult and you don't need any trouble from him. We stick together. We'll come by to get you later for the dinner. Do you want to help in the kitchen?"

"I can take care of myself, Yuri. Just tell me a time.

I'm not a great cook, but I'll give it a try," I said.

"I like your courage. Chopping vegetables is good therapy and we can teach you how to cook."

He stopped eating and stared at my face for a few beats.

"Just be careful."

CHAPTER THREE

I walked out of the bright mess hall and into the dark passageway, where my footsteps clanked on the metal floor with a slight echo. Halfway to my cabin more footsteps indicated that I wasn't alone. I turned to see three crewmen heading my way. They spoke loudly in Russian as they approached. I hugged the wall to let them pass, their loud voices fading as they continued down the corridor.

When I turned to head back to my cabin, I was startled by a face.

"So… we have some unfinished business," Vlad said.

"I don't think there's anything to discuss. I don't want to fight for money," I said, and took a step back.

"Well, we definitely have a problem," Vlad said, narrowing his eyes.

"Look, I'm just a passenger and have nothing to do with your ship."

"Ah, but that's where you're so wrong. Let's go outside and chat."

Two men then came out of the shadows and pushed me towards the bulkhead door. I wasn't going to be able to fight the three of them in this tight space, so I decided to play along.

We headed out onto the deck, Vlad leading and me sandwiched between his men. Vlad stopped at a red metal container and took a deep breath. Then he turned around to face me. He gave a slight nod to his men and they quickly grabbed me and shoved me down onto my knees.

"I thought we were going to talk," I said.

Vlad kneed me hard in the face. My head snapped back in pain and stars flashed in my vision. I opened my eyes and found my face on the floor. Blood and spittle streamed from my mouth and formed a puddle in front of my face. His henchmen pulled me back to my knees and Vlad pummeled my face with a series of quick jabs. They released me and I collapsed to the ground, barely conscious.

"I hope you enjoyed our little chat," he hissed, with

a final kick to my gut.

The air left my body and I gasped. I drifted in and out of consciousness for a few seconds. I lay on the deck desperate for oxygen, but couldn't force any air back into my lungs. My face numb and swollen, I squeezed my eyes tight and blinked hard trying to stay conscious. I listened to their laughter and footsteps move off into the distance. When the hatch door slammed shut behind them blackness engulfed me.

Pain, sharp and sobering, brought me back. I tried to open my eyes, only to find one was swollen shut. I lifted my head and sat up as a wave of nausea washed over me. I breathed in the cold air and watched the steam puff out and dissipate as I exhaled. After a while the nausea passed and I pushed myself up against a container. My head felt heavy but I stood up, steadied myself, and stumbled to the bulkhead door. I fought off a wave of dizziness as I pushed the door open and stepped inside. I grabbed the railing with both hands and pulled my weight up the stairs until I arrived on the third level. On unsteady legs, I fought another wave of dizziness as I entered my cabin and collapsed onto the bed.

A loud knock at my door startled me. The banging came again, louder and longer. I brought my hand up to my face and winced as I touched my swollen eye. My hand came away sticky with congealed blood. I opened the door and saw Robert. His expression quickly changed to anger.

"What the fuck?"

I took a step back, woozy, and crumpled on the bed. This time when I awoke a cold wet cloth was on my forehead. Robert had cleaned me up and brought Yuri and Garry to my cabin. My head was wrapped in gauze.

Yuri handed me an ice pack for my swollen eye.

"Vlad did this. Right? Did you see their faces? I must know."

"Vlad and a couple of his boys wanted to teach me a lesson for picking sides. They held me down while Vlad worked me over." I held the ice pack to my puffed eye.

"I knew it. You should have listened. Vlad is dangerous," Yuri barked, and pounded his fist on my small table.

"I've had worse, like when I was beaten into a coma by a Russian mobster in New York." I said, "I'd like to challenge Vlad to a fight. I might have a chance, one on one."

Yuri gave me a glare and narrowed his eyes.

"There's no fair fighting against Vlad," Garry said, in a quiet voice.

"We will make arrangements for you, but you must rest," Yuri said. "To fight Vlad you must be in top shape, and not with a busted head. In a few days we will reach the first port."

"When is the next fight night?" I asked.

"It's tomorrow, but you're hurt. It's unlikely that Vlad will fight you. He'll pick someone else to represent him. If he does that, I'll fight for you," Yuri said, proudly.

"I'll just have to piss him off so he'll fight me."

CHAPTER FOUR

Yuri and the Belinsky brothers were spot-on about Vlad. I had completely underestimated his dangerous intentions. I felt anger rise from the pit of my stomach as I realized this ship was another war zone. If Vlad knew about the cash and weapons in my cabin. I probably wouldn't be alive for long. I had to get under his skin and get him to focus on fighting me instead of tracking me. I only had to survive a few more days before we arrived at the first port.

"Come on let's get back to the kitchen. We have work to do," Yuri said.

"You come with us. It's not safe for you to be alone anymore," Garry said, in his usual low tone.

"Yes, it is decided. You come now!" Yuri demanded.

We left my cabin and headed down the passageway back to the kitchen. Somewhere in the back of my mind I suspected that there might be an ambush, but the dark corridor was empty. It was the calm before the storm and I could feel the tension rising in all of us.

We reached the mess hall and I sat in a chair watching as the guys prepared dinner. They laughed and joked in Russian. Robert's translations were funnier than the actual jokes and I awkwardly laughed along.

While I sat there, I drifted into my thoughts of New York and all I had lost. Flashes of faces and death filled me with emotion. My first murder was brutal, seeing Manny's face as he suffocated, with a plastic bag over his head. Raven-haired beauty, Angelica, as she strutted down the street, a briefcase filled with money in her hand, seconds before her life ended in a fiery explosion. A pan caught fire, flared, and brought me back to the kitchen.

"Did you have a nice trip?" Yuri asked, as he poured more wine into the pan that again burst into flames for a quick second before the alcohol burned off.

"Sorry, just thinking of home."

The fluidity of the teamwork was amazing. They passed ingredients between each other and crafted a mouth-watering three-course meal. The aroma of garlic, onion, and red wine filled the small room. I stood up to help, but immediately felt a head rush and stumbled back into my chair. I brought my hand up to my face and felt my swollen eye. I winced in pain and took in a deep breath and let it out slowly. My eye seemed to pulse with it's own heartbeat, but the dizziness passed. Robert handed me a warm piece of buttered bread.

"I'm gonna have to pass on that, man. I'm not feeling great. Maybe in a bit."

"Okay, partner."

"You're still not up to snuff yet?" Yuri asked.

"I just need some time to come back to myself. Still feeling a bit unsteady."

Garry came over with a cold wet towel filled with ice, placed it in my hand, and guided it to my swollen face.

"You keep this here on your face, it will help."

The icy towel felt cool and refreshing. The

numbing cold immediately made the throbbing stop and the pain fade.

After a few minutes of holding the cold towel on my cheek, I felt better.

The meal was perfectly timed. Just as they finished preparations, the mess hall began to fill with hungry crewmen. Yuri barked out orders as the team rapidly served dinner. I left the kitchen and sat at the same table where I had lunch. Vlad and his henchmen entered and took their table. We traded glances, but I ignored their laughter and gestures in my direction.

One thug came over, leaned on my table and glared at me. I looked down at his black fingernails dirty with grime and slowly placed a roll on my plate. I wiped at my tearing swollen eye with the back of my hand and winced from the tender bruise.

"Your face looks like shit. You really need to see the doctor," he said, and laughed under his breath.

I could feel his hot breath only inches from my face. Another guy stepped around behind me and waited for a signal from Vlad. I lashed out first in a blur and knocked the closest guy's arms away. His face bounced off the metal table with a loud thud and in a split second I swung my feet around and kicked the other thug off his feet. He struggled to prop himself up, but I kneed him in the forehead. His head snapped back off the wall and all went silent except for my panting.

Yuri rushed out of the kitchen only to find me back in my seat chewing a buttered roll. The two men groaned in pain and tried to recover. Vlad stood abruptly and scowled with a clenched jaw.

Garry then came out of the kitchen and placed a plate of hot rolls on Vlad's table. The two thugs stumbled over and plopped down holding their heads. Vlad looked at his injured men in disgust. He raised his hand in a "gun" gesture and pulled the trigger.

I marched over to confront him in an adrenaline-fueled rage. I stared straight into his eyes.

"Little girls shouldn't play with guns, asshole. Are you so scared that you can't fight me without your friends?"

He shoved me away with both hands.

"I'll fight you tomorrow night. Prepare for pain,"

he hissed, and took off.

"Good luck. I hope things work out for you and your girlfriends," I called after him.

We finished the dinner session and I helped clean up the dining room as Yuri scrubbed the kitchen.

"Where did you learn to fight like that?" Garry asked, as he wiped down a table.

"I spent some time in the military," I said.

"Yeah, those were some slick moves. I like that leg sweep," Robert said as he mopped the floor.

An expression of concern came over Yuri's face.

"Vlad may seem small, but he's a Sambo expert. If he gets you on the ground he'll break a limb," he said.

"I can handle myself, don't worry about me. Just make sure his pals don't cheat. That's the only thing that could give him an unfair advantage."

"This is not a game, my friend. Vlad has killed before," Yuri said.

"We'll do our best, but he's very tricky and probably won't need help," Robert said.

I needed to get off this ship in one piece and get to Viktor, but I wasn't going to let this weasel get the best of me.

CHAPTER FIVE

We finished cleaning the kitchen, shut the lights, and headed down the passageway to the deck. Robert cracked open the bulkhead door and we stepped out into the frozen night. A biting blast of cold air took my breath away and we were greeted by the blackest sky I'd ever seen. Brush strokes of stars made for an astronomer's fantasy.

We headed to the other side of the ship where the containers would shield us from the wind. Yuri leaned back against a blue container and slid to the floor. He pulled out a pack of Lucky Strike cigarettes and lit one up. Robert handed him a bottle of vodka and he took two large gulps before passing it back. Robert then took a quick sip and handed the bottle to me. I drank quickly, feeling the clean burn of the vodka as it went down, and passed the bottle to Garry.

"Vlad plays dirty and will do anything to win," Garry said. "Yuri's beaten everyone Vlad's put against him, but this is his ship and there's no way of knowing what he'll do next." He took another swig.

"There has to be a way to stop him. Why do you guys put up with this crap? I mean, surely you could speak to Captain Kozlov and get him off the ship?"

"Vlad is tightly connected with the family that owns this ship. His uncle sits on the board of the corporation, which means he owns the ship. Even the captain wouldn't go against him for fear of losing his job," Yuri added.

"This is crazy. His ship? C'mon, I thought he was full of shit."

"Well, that's not completely true, but let's just say he could make things very difficult for us," Robert said, then took a drag of his cigarette.

"Why don't you guys just leave?" I asked.

"We would starve before finding another ship job. There are thousands of men waiting for this work," Yuri replied.

"You guys run a great kitchen. Maybe start your own restaurant?" I offered.

"That's our dream, but it takes money we don't

have. For now, we just keep things floating and save our rubles," Yuri snickered, sarcastically.

"I can help you guys and give you money for your business, if you help me with a job outside Moscow. You could leave this shit behind and have the life you've dreamed of. Let's talk about it later."

"You hardly know us. Why would you help?" Robert balked.

"I'm a good judge of character. Besides, you guys are like me. Victims in a game that's out of our control."

"Cooking is my passion, but hunting is my gift," Robert boasted.

"My brother's an expert hunter and I'm a tracker," Garry added.

"When we were kids, we never went hungry. The forest was our playground," Robert said.

Garry gazed into the distance.

"Robert and I grew up in Kiev, but we spent our summers in the Goloseevsky forest. Both our parents worked in a metal factory and saved every penny for summer vacations. We would go up in the mountains to a small lake cabin that had been passed down for generations. The entire family looked forward to our time together fishing and hunting. Mom and Dad cooked delicious meals from whatever we caught. Mom taught us how to cook using herbs and vegetables to add flavor.

"Eventually we got bored fishing and started to hunt squirrels and rabbits. Dad gave us rifles and each day he took us deep into the woods for training on how to live off the land.

"We gradually started hunting larger game like deer and bear. Reading tracks became my thing and I learned to read the forest floor like a book, each track and broken branch had a story.

"On one occasion tracks led us to a whole deer family, a doe and two young fawns. We watched in wonderment as the buck came home and rejoined his family. It was much like our family. They touched noses and nuzzled in caring gestures. We could feel the love between them and so we decided not to kill the buck and his family, but let them live in peace.

"When I was twelve and Robert was fifteen we

came back after a hunting session to find a horrible scene. Our cabin was burned and our parents butchered, their bodies naked and bloody on the shore that they had loved.

"The tracks were easy to follow and led two miles away to a logging campsite. We could hear men's voices filled with laughter. Silently we watched and listened as four men sat around the campfire going through our possessions. When their fire died out we snuck into their camp and slaughtered them in their sleep."

Garry's story stopped when without warning an ear-piercing siren startled us. Yuri yelled in Russian and we hurried inside.

"What's that alarm?" I asked.

"Fire down below. Let's go!" Robert shouted.

We rushed through the bulkhead door and into a passageway filled with heavy smoke. An orange glow lit up the corridor with thick black smoke that bellowed from the kitchen. Crewmen ran past me with hoses that were attached to the ship's walls. Once the fire was extinguished we cleaned and salvaged what we could and stayed up all night until the kitchen functioned again.

None of us said a word as we served the morning meal. We all knew who started the fire and why. It was a twisted message from a tormented mind.

CHAPTER SIX

After breakfast we cleaned up and headed outside for a smoke break. The cold air felt good after the long night without sleep and the busy morning.

I leaned against the railing and watched the waves rise and fall, churning into white caps as the bright blue sky met the tumultuous ocean.

Yuri slapped me on the back.

"You've done well in the kitchen. I thank you for pitching in. Now you know just how insane Vlad is to burn down his own ship to make a point."

"That's right, asshole!" a voice growled behind us.

Vlad glared at us, four of his henchmen with him. One hulking thug with a shaved head and arms thicker than my legs towered over the others. He wasn't as tall as Yuri, but wide and thick like a refrigerator, his neck and arms covered in tattoos.

"Nice work last night, Vlad. Your mother should be proud," I taunted.

He ignored me. Instead, he walked up to the railing, whispered into Yuri's ear, and walked away again.

The refrigerator guy gave Yuri a snarl, which sounded like a dog growling, then followed Vlad and the others back inside.

"What was that?" I asked.

He spoke through clenched teeth. "Vlad wants us all off the ship at the next stop. He burned down my kitchen to show his power."

"Can he really do that?" I asked.

"Yes, once he speaks to his connections," Robert said.

"He must've hidden that guy on the ship for me to fight tonight in the pit. I've never seen him before, but he'll go down just like the others. Every man has his weakness and Vlad does too. It's only a matter of finding it and using it against him," Yuri said.

We smoked in silence, each of us locked in his own thoughts. I knew Vlad would cheat tonight, but wasn't sure how.

"Do you and Garry ever fight?" I asked Robert.

"No, Garry and I coach Yuri and keep outside

influences from interfering as best we can."

"I'm sorry about your family. It must've been horrible growing up without parents."

"It's made us stronger. We've always watched out for each other." Robert reflected, and took a long drag of his cigarette.

I heard footsteps coming our way again. One of the captain's stewards appeared from around the corner of a container and spoke fast in Russian. He pivoted quickly and headed back towards the tower.

"What is it?" I asked.

"The captain wants us in his control room. Now," Garry said.

CHAPTER SEVEN

We entered the control room where Captain Kozlov sat with his back to the door. He rubbed his face and shook his head as he turned to face us. A bottle of vodka and four glasses waited for us on his navigation table.

"Something unfortunate has come up. I'm being forced to release you at the next port and I don't fucking like it," he scowled.

He poured vodka into the glasses, and then drank straight out of the bottle as he motioned for us to drink.

Yuri patted the captain's back. "Don't worry, old friend. It is not worth losing your command over."

"What's our first port?" I asked.

"Southampton," the captain replied.

"How much time do we have?"

"Tomorrow night."

"That only leaves us one choice," I said. "Vlad has

to have an accident."

"He's far too smart for that. Besides he's always guarded. The only chance is during the fight tonight," Garry offered.

"Well then it's up to me or we all get booted at Southampton. If we're even alive when we get there," I said.

The captain poured more vodka and we drank it down.

"I'll call my New York connections. I may have a place for us to stay in Ireland," I said.

"We don't even have enough money to get us home," Robert said.

"I will help once we arrive."

"Good luck tonight, my friends," the captain said, and he grabbed the bottle off the table and gazed out the ship's front window.

We headed back to the kitchen to prepare dinner. Once the meal was served and the crew ate, we cleaned up and got ready for the fights. Robert held pads up for Yuri to practice his punches. I started to become mesmerized by the rhythm of the sounds as

Yuri's fists came in contact with the pads.

Garry came and sat beside me on the floor. "They do this before every fight. Helps keep him loose. Can I help you?"

"Thanks, but I have my own methods. Hey, I'm sorry about your parents. That was an awful story." I said, "Such a waste of life."

"Thanks for your kind words, Bill. It still haunts me to this day." Then he quickly changed the subject. "Have you been in a pit before?"

"Not exactly, but I've had many confrontations. Are there any rules?" I asked.

"No. The faster the fight ends, the better off you are."

"Can you show me the place? I want to see the layout."

"Sure, it's down near the boiler room." He motioned to Yuri. "I'm going to take Bill down to see the fighting area."

"Hold on we're coming," Yuri said. "We should stay together." He picked up a towel and wiped sweat off his face and neck.

We headed down a set of stairs towards the engine room. The ship creaked and swayed as we made our way deeper. The air became dank and the engine grew louder as we descended.

The fight area was much smaller than I thought it would be, a little bigger than the mess hall. It was going to be tight, which made it even more dangerous.

Then Yuri entered a dark room and hit a switch. Bright overhead fluorescent lights flooded the space with a bluish tint. The room had doors on both sides. I walked into the center and started my katas. Each form had a unique combination of punches, blocks, and kicks. I moved fluidly through my routine as I'd done a thousand times before. After about twenty minutes, I'd centered myself and then sat on the floor with eyes closed, completely satisfied and ready.

Someone clapped and I opened my eyes.

"Very impressive."

It was Vlad, along with the human refrigerator and four other henchmen. They strolled confidently into the room with two-foot long lead pipes in their hands. One guy smacked his pipe into his hand. He took a step closer and glared at me.

"It's time for your second lesson," Vlad hissed.

"Okay so no event tonight? Too bad, cause I was hoping to place some big money on our fight," I said. The tension grew thicker with each passing second.

"Oh you have money, huh?" Vlad asked.

"The captain is gonna be disappointed missing out on all this fun. I heard he's a big spender."

"How about this, smart guy? Once I beat your head in, I'll take all your money."

The four thugs came a few steps closer each bearing a similar expression of evil determination to hurt us and break our bones.

I felt something stir inside me, a coldness beyond reason, something dark I recognized from my past. It roared closer like a freight train inside my head. I'd used this anger before, and I knew what was coming.

My eyes darted from man to man and quickly I reached into the back of my waistband and pulled out a Glock 19. *Pow! Pow!* The sound of the shots echoed loudly, like firecrackers going off. In seconds, two of Vlad's men were writhing on the ground in excruciating pain, holding their legs and bleeding profusely. Their pipes clattered to the floor and Vlad's other henchmen took a step back. Vlad's bulky friend moved towards me and seemed to regret that move when I pointed my gun at his face.

"You got something to say?" I taunted.

Vlad fumed, his face red with rage and his fists clenched. The oversized thug stood stupefied, mouth open, and seeming to not know what to do next. Vlad turned and stomped out.

The smell of cordite and smoke filled the room. My ears slowly stopped ringing and the sound was replaced by the moans of Vlad's fallen comrades. If Vlad had a gun he would've used it. Clearly the shit was rising and the next wave of violence could only escalate.

"Wow! That was fucking amazing?" Robert cheered.

"You are one whacked-out dude. I didn't know you had a gun. That saved us for now." Yuri said.

CHAPTER EIGHT

Yuri used the ship's intercom system to summon the ship's doctor. He arrived a few minutes later, a cigarette hanging from his mouth, with two men carrying a stretcher. A sloppy mess of a man in his sixties, bald and chunky, he dropped a large black leather medical bag on the floor and began to work on the injured men. Once he'd patched one up, he barked at his helpers to carry the injured to sick bay, and he went to work on the other. Soon the helpers returned and carried the second injured man away.

At that, the doctor walked over to Yuri and shouted at him in Russian. Yuri yelled back and the doctor immediately stopped to look at me. He took a few steps closer, gave me a slight smirk, and patted my back.

"Good job. I never thought anyone could shut Vlad up. I'm glad to see someone finally gave him a go."

He lit another cig off the embers of his filter. Ash fell onto his belly and then to the floor, but he didn't seem to notice or care. A cloud of smoke surrounded his head and eventually overtook the smell of cordite. He picked up his bag and headed out.

I thought about my journey to kill Viktor and I knew I desperately needed their help. There was no way of knowing what I was facing or how powerful Viktor's brother was. I had to convince Yuri to help me by letting him in on my past and my future plans. I never had my own crew, but if their abilities turned out to be real we'd be a seriously dangerous crew. "Let's go to my cabin. There are some things about my situation you guys should know."

When we got upstairs, I unlocked the door and we all crammed into the tiny room.

"What's this all about?" Yuri asked, and sat on the small table.

Robert and Garry sat on my bed and waited.

I pulled out the two large carryall bags from the closet and dropped them at their feet. They looked down at the bags and then up at me, confused. I unzipped the first bag and pulled it open.

"That's a fucking crazy arsenal. What are you doing with all those weapons?" Robert asked.

"Wait. Are those grenades? What are you, some kind of terrorist?" Garry asked.

Yuri's face was unreadable, so I continued. I unzipped the other bag, exposing bundles of U.S. dollars.

"I used to work for a New York criminal organization, but my life took a bad turn when my partner double crossed me. He teamed up with a greedy Russian gangster to fuck me over. I was beaten into a coma and in the end I was duped into thinking that my girlfriend was kidnapped, but my partner had stolen her away while I was out of commission. To make matters even worse, I found out my partner was a FBI agent. The gangster fled to Moscow where his brother is a powerful kingpin. I'm going to hunt him down, then go home and take care of my old partner."

I paused and waited for them to respond, but they just stared at the bags at their feet.

"So, you guys wanna be in my crew? What do you

say? I'll fund your restaurant in New York City after Viktor Tsapok is dead."

They all remained quiet.

"Each of you take a weapon and let's make it off this ship alive."

Robert dug into the bag and pulled out two combat knives. He held them up to the light and examined them. The light reflected off the sharp edges. He placed them down then reached back into the bag. He handed Yuri a black Berretta 9mm.

"I don't need a gun, I'm my own weapon," Yuri scowled.

"I'll take it then." Garry snatched the 9mm from Robert.

"What is the brother's name in Moscow?" Yuri questioned.

"Boris Tsapok. Do you know him?" I asked, hopeful.

"No, but I know who to ask."

It was the first sign that Yuri was on board to help me find Viktor. I gave him a slight nod then zipped up the bags and put them away.

"I'll call my New York contacts when we get to port. They have friends in Ireland who can help us. The only thing in our way now is Vlad."

CHAPTER NINE

As we headed back down to the engine room, I heard loud voices of men laughing and talking. We stepped into the room and to my surprise it was completely packed with people. The captain greeted us in Russian, with another full bottle of vodka, but his voice was drowned out by the noise of the others. It looked like the whole ship was attending the pit fight and I couldn't help but wonder who was in control of the ship.

Vlad eventually showed up with his bulky friend, and placed a gym bag on the floor. The crowd went instantly quiet as Vlad walked to the center and raised his hands over his head. He scanned the room and we locked eyes. His face remained expressionless as he glared in my direction. He turned and shouted in Russian, while he pointed at me. The audience roared at whatever he said.

"What's going on? What did he say?"

"He's claiming 3-1 odds that they will win both fights," Garry explained.

"What's the max bet they will cover?"

"Three hundred thousand rubles about five thousand U.S."

"Are they good for it?" I asked.

"The captain holds the money, so it's always fair."

Everyone in the room hollered and offered their bets. Fistfuls of cash exchanged hands. A small man took the bets and scribbled them into a notepad. After about ten minutes of yelling and betting everyone settled down.

Now Vlad raised his hands again, this time to announce that there would be only two fights tonight. The first would be Vlad's hulk against Yuri. The room became filled with an electric tension as Vlad paused for effect. The noise became louder as everyone joined in and heckled the men as they entered the center.

The men stepped into the center and took off their shirts. Yuri began jumping around and punched at the air to warm up. He did a couple of squats and stretched out his arms and legs, and rotated his head in a circle. His neck made an audible crack that I heard from a few feet away. Vlad's man stood arms out in front of him ready to grab Yuri, his eyes wide with excitement and anticipation.

"Attention. Attention!" Vlad called out and the noise settled down to a murmur. He turned to me with a smirk. He then started barking out Russian words in short bursts. The crowd listened intently and then a loud roar filled the room. Vlad pointed at the big man and introduced him as Brent McGill from Scotland, and spit out his fighting credentials in Russian as more bets were placed.

"This is no good," Robert grunted.

"What's no good?" I asked.

"He said both fights will take place at the same time," Garry added.

Yuri's face remained unchanged and focused on Brent McGill.

"Here, place this on us to win," I said, and handed Garry a wad of cash - five thousand U.S. dollars.

"This is crazy. Are you sure?"

"Just do it."

Garry rushed up to the bet taker and handed him the stack of bills. The bet taker whispered into Vlad's ear the amount needed to cover the odds and he handed a paper bag of cash to the bookie. He looked into Vlad's bag and nodded that the money was there, and then placed it into the canvas bag along with his notepad. He handed the whole bundle to the captain and with that the betting was closed.

CHAPTER TEN

Vlad took off his shirt and pumped his fists into the air to rally the crowd. His body was without an ounce of fat. Corded, defined muscles danced under his blue-green tattoos, which covered his neck, arms, and chest. The ink at the center of his chest had a portrait of a beautiful woman, her eyes slightly Asian, with dark hair that flowed around her neck and down Vlad's stomach. It morphed near his navel into a snake's head with a gapping maw of fangs with dripping venom. Another massive tattoo with an image of the *Eilbek* dramatically crashing through ocean waves covered his back.

Vlad pounded his chest and roared a primal scream. Spittle flew from his mouth and I felt a chill go down my spine.

Yuri held his fists up and nodded and the fight started. Vlad and Brent bum rushed me before I was ready, but I managed to duck Brent's wild swings at my head. Yuri quickly scurried to my aid and pulled Brent away. Unfortunately, Vlad came in low and tackled me. He wrapped both his arms around my thighs, lifted me up off the ground, and slammed me on my back. I went down hard, my spine and head taking most of the impact. A sharp, white-hot pain flashed through my head and for a few seconds I had no air in my lungs.

Vlad pushed his knees passed my hips, mounted my stomach with lightning speed, then systematically launched a barrage of fists and elbows to my head. I managed to block some of his blows with my forearms and bucked desperately to shake him off my chest, but he hooked his legs under my thighs and locked them in place. I feebly grabbed at the back of his head and pulled his face down to my chest, but he reared up and broke free. My attempts to hold him down only kept him from pummeling me for a few seconds before he broke free again and continued his attack. I needed to turn the tide if I was going to last, but he was just too fast and strong on the ground.

I glanced over at Yuri for help and he quickly

shuffled over and kicked Vlad's head. The impact made a loud thud and knocked Vlad's head sideways at such a grotesque angle, I thought Yuri had broken his neck. Vlad's eyes rolled back in his head and he released my thighs.

I rolled him over and took the top position. I finally caught my breath. Vlad's face was now an open target. I smashed him with a series of elbows and followed up with a head butt. Blood flowed and soaked both our faces. At first I wasn't sure whose blood it was until I stuck my thumb into a deep cut on Vlad's brow. Blood trickled down into his eyes and he blinked rapidly in an effort to regain his eyesight.

Vlad threw out his hands and tried to block my assault, but we were both too slick for him to grab hold of my hands. Desperate to protect his face he rolled over onto his stomach and I had his back. I slipped my arms under his face and sunk my forearms in deep under his chin and around his neck. I began to squeeze and tighten my grip to cut off his air. Vlad gasped and slapped at my closed fists and tried to pry them open, but I wouldn't let go. Too stubborn to surrender, he bucked and twisted until he went slack, unable to breathe. I released him, relieved by my win. Until he rolled over, stood to face me, and swung a wild roundhouse punch that missed. He wiped wildly at his eyes to clear his vision, and then lunged at me, but I jumped back.

I glanced over to see Yuri and Brent locked in a clinch. They grappled for control, each body punch connected with a grunt and a sickening crack. They weren't bloody like Vlad and I, but both had swollen, puffed-up faces. A salty, metallic flavor saturated my mouth and I spit out a wad of bloody phlegm.

The crowd cheered as the sparring resumed.

I had to make sure the fight didn't go to the ground again. Vlad's ground skills were too strong and I definitely couldn't afford to give him that advantage. I threw a few jabs that rocked his head back. Then finished a combination with an upper cut that missed.

He dashed in, gripped my upper body, and dropped down to sweep at my legs, but I sprawled out and threw both legs back to keep him from gaining control.

We fell to the ground as he pulled me down on top of him. Then he reached into his pants and his finger came out full of white powder. He rubbed his hand across my face and my eyes, which immediately burned as if they were on fire. Huge tears dripped from my eyes as I frantically tried to clear my vision, but the burning was overwhelming.

I burst from my position and swung around. I took his arm and pulled it between my legs. As I straightened it, I kept the pressure on. Vlad flipped his whole body and tried to roll out, but I yanked back harder until I heard a loud snap. He screamed in pain and crumpled into a ball, cradling his arm. I jumped on top of him and rained down blows until he collapsed, unconscious.

I knelt down and wiped at my burning eyes, trying to see what was happening in Yuri's fight. Unconscious and stiff, Vlad lay with his head back and took short, sputtering breaths. The doctor hurried over and checked Vlad's eyes and breathing. He reached into his bag for smelling salts, and Vlad was jolted back to consciousness, though seemingly confused about where he was and what was going on. Within minutes, he was carried away on a stretcher.

The doctor then turned his attention to me, wiping my eyes with wet gauze that felt cool and refreshing. I then heard a loud, wet smack that brought my attention back to Yuri's fight. It was hard to tell who was winning.

"That's enough!" Yuri barked.

"You're taking a piss!" Brent declared.

"Aren't you tired of this?" Yuri asked.

"Why don't you give up?"

"Nyet," Yuri said, and launched himself at Brent.

He spun around and jumped on his back, and pulled Brent's arm across his neck and shoulder in a sleeper hold. Brent swung around wildly, but it was no use. Yuri used Brent's own right arm to cut off the blood supply to his brain and tightened his grip. Both of them fell to ground and Yuri still managed to hold on while Brent gasped for air. Eventually Brent stopped moving and the fight was finished.

I ran over, picked up one of Brent's arms, and watched as it flopped to the floor. I smacked Yuri's back to try and make him stop before it became fatal.

"It's over, he's done," I said.

Brent was out cold, his breath slow and even. Yuri's right eye was swollen shut. A black and blue mark had already started forming around a cut on his face.

He nodded.

"Yeah. We did it!" he screamed, and pulled my hand up in triumph.

Robert and Garry lifted me up and carried me around the room on their shoulders.

"We did it! We did it!" they cheered.

"Good job, boys. That was one crazy fight," Garry said.

"Fucking awesome!" Robert added.

The captain then came over with the money bag, but I could tell something was wrong.

"Extremely entertaining boys. We've paid out the bets to the crew and here's what's left. There's only one problem," he said, a pained expression on his face.

"What's the problem?" I asked.

"Vlad's money to cover your bet was just paper.

Not a single dollar. I guess he was sure he'd win. Sorry, guys."

I felt sick. Anger welled up from the pit of my stomach. The jubilation I felt was quickly quashed and I wanted to march down to sickbay and pound Vlad some more.

"What a fucking waste. I should've known something was up when the bet taker looked into Vlad's money bag."

"Why's that?" Robert asked.

"I saw him give Vlad a look," I said.

"It doesn't matter now. We beat him," Yuri said.

"Yeah, but they ripped us off," Robert said.

"Well at least we took a piece of Vlad's pride. He'll be nursing that arm for a long time," I said.

I touched my own beat-up face, which felt tight and puffy and thanks to the doctor's gauze, smelled heavily of alcohol and peroxide.

The doctor returned and examined the top of my head and a cut in my hairline.

"You're gonna need a few stitches for that one. Come to my office later and I'll take care of it."

He then peered up at Yuri.

"I can't reach you up there, kneel down," he demanded.

Yuri obeyed. "How's this?"

"Much better."

The doctor pressed medicine into the wound under Yuri's eye with a cotton swab.

Yuri gave no indication whether the medicine burned.

"Listen, Yuri, you have to get this new guy off this ship," he said, gesturing in my direction. "I came here to keep busy until I could retire, not open up a new practice. I haven't worked this hard in years and I don't want to. Do you understand?"

"Vlad wants us off at the next port anyway," I offered.

"Perfect."

The doctor then picked up his case and returned to sickbay. The crewmen emptied out with grumbles from money lost on Vlad's team. Only a few left counting their winnings.

"Vlad will probably come after us once he recovers.

I can't imagine he'll let us walk off the ship without some kind of payback," Robert said.

"I just hope we don't have to shoot our way off this ship," Garry added.

"Let's get my head stitched up and see the mood in sickbay," I said.

"I don't care what the mood is, I'll shoot my way off this ship if I have to," Robert growled.

CHAPTER ELEVEN

Robert seemed extremely jumpy as we headed to sickbay. I wasn't sure if it was because he carried a gun, or that he might have to use it. Vlad was out cold on a cot sleeping off his injuries. The doctor pushed me into a seat by a table and stitched me up.

"How's Vlad?" I asked.

"Vlad was in pain, so I gave him something to help him rest," he said, and held his finger to his lips.

Yuri and the doctor then whispered to each other in Russian.

"What going on?" I asked.

"The doctor says that Vlad's fine. His memory loss was only temporary and when he found out how the fight ended he was angry. I'm not sure how long the doctor can help us."

"It is best that we get off the ship before a war breaks out. I don't want to shoot anyone this week," Robert said, and gave me a smirk.

"Besides, Bill has some work lined up for us," Garry said.

We thanked the doctor and made our way back to my cabin. Once inside I dumped the winnings out on the bed. We counted the mix of currencies, which equaled a little over $1,300, U.S.

"What a joke," I growled.

"At least no one died. It would've been really bad for us if we lost. There's no way of knowing what Vlad could've done to us," Garry said.

"True," Yuri said.

"Let's go outside and discuss the plan," I said.

I locked up the cabin and we marched down the stairs and stepped out onto the deck.

I pulled up my jacket collar against the cold win and fired up a smoke.

"I'm open to suggestions, but here's my plan. I'll reach out to my New York connections and get us a contact in Ireland. Then we'll stock up on supplies and head over to Kiev," I said.

"I know people there who will help us find these Russian gangsters. My sister runs a small bed and breakfast where we can stay. The Daisy B&B Hotel, just outside Kyiv City."

"Oh, the princess, right? What's her name?" I asked, and took a drag of my cig.

"Ha ha, very funny. Her name is Julia and she's a few years younger than me."

I could see the love in his face as he drifted into his own thoughts. A great sadness came over me as I thought about home and my lost love. As I searched off into the distance, I noticed a group of islands appear on the horizon. I took a few more drags of my cigarette before the wind burned it down to the filter. I tossed the butt over the side and left the guys to talk to the captain.

"There's my new champion," the captain said, with a smile as I entered the control room.

I smiled back. "How long before we dock?"

"You made me some nice money, my friend. Let's drink," he said, and shoved a glass of vodka into my hand.

"Are you going to have trouble with Vlad after we leave?" I asked.

"There's always trouble with Vlad. I'm going to call the corporation when we get to port. His criminal activities have to be stopped. Hopefully they'll at least hear me out. If they don't like what I have to say, fuck them. I'm tired of this shit." He knocked back his shot and slammed the glass on the table.

"I appreciate all your help, but there's no way I'll be able to get back on this ship again."

"That is true. But I don't think it's the end of your Vlad troubles."

I left the captain's control room and headed back down to my cabin to pack. I was horrified to find my lock bent and broken. I pushed the door open and found one of my black carryall bags unzipped on the bed. Shock and anger overwhelmed me. Vlad was out cold in the sick bay. How could this be? I ran my hand down the damaged locker. The metal door had been bent with some kind of heavy-duty tool. My guns and money were gone and all that was left was clothes and cigarettes. I rubbed at my face and dropped down on the bed.

"How could I be so stupid?" I thought.

I tried to get a grip and gather myself. All I had now was the gun in my waistband and the cash from the fight in my pockets. I had more money in the bank, but half my funds and my entire arsenal were lost.

I packed up what was left of my things and made my way down to the mess hall to speak with Yuri and Belinsky brothers. When I told them what had happened in my room Yuri turned red and jumped to his feet.

"Let's go!" he barked.

We followed Yuri to Vlad's cabin where eight bunks were stacked in a small room against the walls. In the center of the room, a group of crewmen smoked, drank, and played cards. Yuri stormed in and Brent stood up to block his way. I leaned around the two massive men and noticed my black bag on a bunk in the corner. The bookie from the fight sat next to the open bag and was placing the cash into small piles.

"That doesn't belong to you," Yuri barked.

"You're gonna have to take it, mate," Brent growled, puffing out his chest.

He went to reach for something in his waistband,

but before the sentence was finished Yuri was on him. One fast punch hit Brent's gut and he collapsed to his knees, gasping for air.

Yuri stepped over Brent, who continued to hack and gasp.

"You've taken our friend's hard-earned possessions. Now give it all back before this gets ugly."

The bet taker shrank back on the bed and started to stuff the money into the black bag. He froze in fear as Yuri's shadow engulfed him.

"I was just following orders, Yuri. C'mon, you know what it's like. Right?"

"Sure, I completely understand."

Yuri drilled him in the face and his head bounced off the metal wall. His eyes rolled back in his head and he slumped lifelessly to the floor. The bookie stared at the ceiling unconscious as a trickle of blood rolled from the corner of his mouth.

The card players watched in silence. Yuri grabbed the bag, zipped it up, and stepped over Brent. He stopped, turned back, and reached into Brent's waistband for the pistol.

"You won't be needing this, mate," he said, and tucked it into the front of his pants.

We met each other's eyes and I gave him a nod of gratitude. I noticed something suddenly change in Yuri's face. A grim expression came over him. I turned around to see Vlad standing behind Robert and Garry with an AK-47 assault rifle. He held the weapon with one hand, while the other hung in a blue sling from his neck. Vlad could've easily turned us into a bloody mess with a flick of his finger.

"Drop the fuckin' bag and get out," he whispered, with eyes glassy and a finger on the trigger.

He took a few steps back and waved his rifle for us to follow Yuri out. Yuri looked down at the bag.

"Just do it," Vlad growled.

Yuri sighed, dropped the bag.

"We'll be docking in a couple of hours, make sure you're all off. If I see any of you again I'll feed you to the sharks," Vlad said through clenched teeth.

"It's not your bag," Yuri said, moving towards Vlad.

He pointed the rifle up into Yuri's face and pressed the barrel hard against his cheek.

"So honorable and so stupid. Don't you ever learn? I always win. Now get the fuck out," he snarled.

Vlad pressed the rifle harder into Yuri's cheek, and scraped the nozzle off his skin leaving an angry red abrasion.

"That bag doesn't belong to you," Robert tried.

"Everything on this ship belongs to me. Brent, get the fuck up and take their weapons!" Vlad ordered.

Brent stumbled to his feet and patted Yuri down. When he found his gun in Yuri's waistband, he yanked it out then whipped it across Yuri's face. Yuri didn't flinch or move. The only sign of the impact was a trickle of blood that ran down the side of his face from a thin cut over his right eye.

Brent aggressively took all our guns. The card-playing crewmen stood up and made sure that we left without causing any additional trouble. Any hope of overpowering Vlad faded once our weapons were confiscated.

"Now you can leave," Vlad said.

He took a step back and motioned with his rifle towards the exit. The bet taker shuffled over, picked up the black bag, and brought it back to his bunk. Pure rage welled up inside of me as I watched him empty the bag again. I wanted to kill them all, but I was completely powerless.

"If anyone of you are still on this ship after we leave the next port you'll be turned into chum. Now get out of my sight!"

CHAPTER TWELVE

I stood on the deck as we pulled into the Port of Southampton. The crew came on deck and prepared for docking, while Captain Kozlov remained hidden in his control room, clearly embarrassed by his lack of power over the situation.

Once the ramp was adjusted we grabbed what little we were allowed to leave with and walked down the gangplank. I turned to take one last look at the *Eilbek*, feeling both frustrated and free.

The dock was bustling with activity. Enormous cranes lifted forty-foot-long metal containers and placed them like toys onto the waiting decks. Busy dockworkers shouted orders in multiple languages. Forklifts moved crates of supplies from the warehouse to each ship. The black asphalt was a mix of rainbow oil slicks and puddles, and the air was heavy with the scents of ocean water and exhaust fumes.

"As least we're done with that asshole," I said.

"Not yet," said Robert, motioning to three police cars approaching, with red flashing lights on their rooftops. The doors flung open and officers jumped out, batons in hand.

Six men in dark blue uniforms surrounded us. "Hold it right there, fellows. You men are in the custody of the Port of Southampton," one officer yelled.

A parting gift from Vlad, clearly. I knew this had nothing to do with my escape from American otherwise the FBI would've been here, too.

"Stay where you are," an officer said. a scowl on his hard-lined leathery face.

"We'll keep them busy Bill, you try and get yourself out of here. I'll be working with my sister when this is all over." Yuri declared.

He turned and approached the police with hands in the air speaking Russian. Robert and Garry followed his lead.

"I can't just leave you guys. What are you doing?" I asked.

"Take off Bill, we got this." Robert said.

"See you around." Garry said, with a smirk and a shrug.

The other officers held out batons anticipating a situation. Two came in from the right and moved in on Yuri. They tried to contain him, but he kept yelling something with his hands up.

"No English!" he shouted.

When Yuri resisted arrest, three more of the officers moved in and tried to wrestle him to the ground. One jumped onto his back in an unsuccessful effort to throw him off balance. The others rushed in and swung their batons at his legs. Yuri spun around quickly and the officer on his back flew off and landed hard on the pavement, stunned. Robert and Garry joined the fray with a flurry of kicks and punches.

"Stop. No English!" Robert cried.

Garry tried to help Yuri by grabbing one of the officers by the leg. They both tumbled to the ground.

As the brawl continued, I slowly backed up and saw my chance to slip away. I quickly ducked into the nearest open warehouse where supplies were piled high against the walls and were being moved by forklifts into the waiting ships. After a few steps in the opposite direction I borrowed a yellow hard hat to blend in and quickly made it out of the warehouse and onto the street.

A small black taxi approached and I waved it down. The driver pulled to the curb and stopped. I opened the door and hopped in. "Where to, mate?"

"Is there a good place to eat around here?" I asked.

He turned to face me with his arm across the back of the front seat. "Yeah, there's a great pub just a tick away. The Red Lion. One of the oldest pubs in Southampton."

"Great, let's go."

"You here on holiday?"

"Yes, sir. I always wanted to see the UK."

"Most folks go to London, but we get our share of tourists too. Do you need a good place to stay as well?" he asked.

"Why? Do you get a cut?"

"Hah! I wish, mate."

When we arrived at the pub, I reached into my

pocket and pulled out a wad of cash. Thankfully I still had the money I'd won in the fight, which I'd stuffed into my pockets.

The driver pulled the taxi over to the curb and I peered out the window at the pub. The whole block had a historic appearance like buildings locked in time from centuries ago. The stores were two stories high with arches and trim that gave it that old world charm.

I paid the driver, added a few dollars as a tip and climbed out onto the street.

"Here, take my card. Call me anytime you need a ride."

I looked down at the card and read his name was Benny. I'd never had a taxi driver so friendly before, but it was a nice change.

"You can ask anyone in the town about me. I know everyone."

"Thanks, Benny. I'm Bill. I'll definitely give you a call later."

"Brilliant. Cheers, Bill," he said, and pulled away from the curb with a screech.

I picked up my bag and headed into The Red Lion.

It smelled familiar, like bars back home, and an old bartender with white hair combed back immediately greeted me with a nod then glanced at a soccer game on a television mounted on the wall.

"Hey," I said, and looked around.

"Sit wherever you like young man," the bartender said.

He had a red, weathered face, creased with deep wrinkles from years of hard drinking.

He wiped the bar top and chatted with three old men who were also fully engaged in the game. Most of the light in the bar came from the television and fluorescent lights behind a wall of liquor bottles. A group of wooden booths stood opposite the bar and went down the length of the building, which led to bathrooms and a back door.

I sat at a dark wooden booth, placed my bag under the table and looked around for a waitress, but didn't see anyone else working.

"What'll ye be havin'?" the bartender called out.

"A pint of ale, please."

"Coming right up."

After a couple of minutes he placed a mug on the bar and then went back to chatting with the other men. It was immediately clear that this was a self-service establishment. I headed to the bar and leaned in, trying to get his attention to pay for the ale, but everyone was absorbed in the game.

When their team scored, they cheered, and the bartender finally turned his attention back to me.

"You need something else, mate?"

"How much for the ale?"

"Later, just relax. We're busy watching football."

"Okay," I said, and sat and watched the game.

I drank down three inches of the cold ale and wiped the foam off my lip with the back of my hand.

A few minutes later, a group of young men burst loudly into the bar through the back entrance and crowded around.

"Hey, give us a lager!" one shouted.

There were only five of them, though with the noise they made coming in, it sounded like more. They looked disheveled, with stretched-out t-shirts and messy hair. Three were of average build and one was heavyset. A tall, lanky guy with an unhappy look on his face was clearly the leader and shouted again for beers, and then noticed me.

"What the fuck are you lookin' at?" he barked, and spit as he said it.

"Me? Nothing, I'm just enjoying an ale and the game."

"Good. Then fuckin' turn around and mind your own fuckin' business, ye wanker."

"Hold on, Chester," the bartender said. "Don't start bothering my customers again. I'm getting your lagers right now. You boys can take a seat and behave."

"I'll take a fuckin' seat when I'm fuckin' good and ready, old man."

"Hey! Take it easy, man," I said, and stood to face him.

He was easily a head taller then me and stared me down with angry eyes.

"What! Are you takin' a piss? I think this fucking bloke is takin' a piss? What do you boys think?"

"I think he's needin' a lesson," the heavyset one

said.

"So, lookin' for a bit of action are we?" the tall guy taunted, his face reddening.

"C'mon, Chester, cut that shite out. Here's ya beers, he's not looking for any trouble." The bartender placed their lagers on the bar.

He then placed six shot glasses on the bar, grabbed a bottle, and started pouring amber liquid into each glass.

"Here, Chester. Bushmills on the house."

"Alright, alright. Is this a friend of yours, Pete? I don't like the look of him. He smells like he needs a good beatin'." He handed the beers out to his crew.

"I'll come back for you later, maybe we need us a chat outside," he said, and then handed out the shots, except for one, which stayed on the bar. They took a table in the back, but close enough that I could hear their conversation.

"I don't like his face," one of them said.

"Let's give him a proper welcome," another suggested.

"Just drink up and then we'll have us some fun,"

Chester said, with a grin.

I ignored their comments, focused on the game, and enjoyed the elderly men's banter as they twitched with anticipation and tried to will their team to victory.

I heard more loud laughter from the back booths and turned to see Chester snorting white power off the table with a rolled-up bill.

"Here, boys, get in on this. It's fuckin' grand."

He sniffed in deep and wiped his nose with the back of his hand.

They passed the rolled bill around, and then abruptly stopped when the front door swung open. Chester and his crew rushed to get the evidence off the table.

"Hurry up, ya twit."

Chester brushed off the table, and lifted his beer to take a big swig

as a tall police officer stepped into the bar. He took off his hat and placed it in front of him.

"Hello gents. Who's winning today?" he asked, and leaned on the bar with both elbows.

"Good day, Constable Lawson," Pete said.

"Crystal Palace is a bunch of wankers, but Brighton's not finished yet, we're coming back."

"What's going on in here, Pete?" the officer asked, nodding to the hoodlums in the back booths. "I thought I told you beasties not to come around here again. Now, get out before I run you all in."

Three of the crew bolted out the back door leaving Chester and his chubby friend alone. They looked suspiciously nervous, but stayed in their seats.

"Oh I see, rebellious are we?" Constable Lawson said.

He took his hat off the bar, tucked it under his right arm, and walked over to Chester.

As he got closer, the chubby thug struggled out of the booth to get away, but only had time to stand next to his friend.

He glared at them. "What are you boys still doing here?"

The chubby thug took a few steps back and finally managed to escape out the back door.

"You wee shite," Chester growled, as the door slammed shut.

"Nice crew you have, Chester. They can't even tough it out with you."

"Just havin' a cold one. Not harming anyone yet," he said, defiantly.

"Put a move on it, Chester," Constable Lawson said.

He took out his baton and tapped the table twice.

"Okay, mate," Chester said, and slowly drank the rest of his beer before eyeing the Constable and leaving out the back.

"I'm not your mate," Lawson said.

The Constable came back to the bar, looked at me and then at Pete.

"Could I please have a wee bit of ice water, Pete?"

Pete placed the glass before him and the Constable drank half.

"Have you seen any Russian lads come through here today? There was a bit of a ruckus at the port a while ago and it looks like one got away."

"No Russians here today."

I became uneasy, and froze as I thought about Yuri and the boys creating a scene so I could escape. I definitely needed Yuri's help to kill Viktor, but couldn't risk being arrested and sent back home. I knew it was time for me to leave, but I didn't want to seem too obvious, so I waited.

"How about you there?" Now he addressed me.

"Me? I'm from New York. On vacation."

"Ah, New York? On holiday are we? I love your accent. Is that Brooklyn I hear?"

"Manhattan. West side."

"I have to take the misses on a holiday to America one of these days. She's been bugging me relentlessly and wants to see the Empire State Building. You know ride a danglebox all the way to the top like proper tourists. Have you ever been up there?"

"As a kid. It scared the shit out of me. Everything looked like small toys and people looked like ants," I said.

He nodded. "Well, you men have a good day. And hey Pete, if any those little fuckers come around again give us a call. We don't want to wait for another incident on some poor bloke." He finished his water and stood. "Thanks mate."

"Sure, Davie."

He turned to me. "Well, enjoy your holiday... umm. What's your name?"

"John O'Brien. Nice to meet you," I said, and held out my hand.

"Okay, Mister O'Brien," he said, shaking my hand. "Watch out for those hooligans if you're going be around for a while."

After he left, I looked down at the shot of Bushmills whiskey Pete had poured. I picked it up and knocked it back and let out a breath. It had a slight burn and warmed my chest for a few seconds. I needed a few more to calm my nerves after that close call.

CHAPTER THIRTEEN

I settled up with Pete and headed out into the street. The sky took on an orange tint with purple clouds as daylight faded out behind the rows of buildings off in the distance. As I walked the sky morphed into a colorful dark sunset. Decorative black iron streetlights flickered on as dusk settled in.

I looked up the street for another taxi, but found none. The town was pretty empty. I walked east for a bit with the sun on my back, and hoped to find a busier location to hail a ride.

I pulled out Benny's card, and then worked my phone out of my bag only to find it dead. I turned onto Bernard Street and hoped to find a restaurant, maybe someplace where I could get something to eat and charge my phone.

After a few blocks I came to an intersection and noticed an Indian restaurant. The aroma of curry and onions filled my senses and made my stomach growl.

I stepped into the restaurant and was greeted by a friendly Indian woman. She had her hair tied back and wore a patterned turquoise dress and several gold necklaces. After being seated in a booth, I read through the menu and ordered Chicken Tikka Masala, which came with basmati rice and warm Naan. The hot, spicy food hit the spot.

I got another good break and found an outlet under the table to charge my phone. Once my phone was charged, I called Patrick Sullivan, my past boss in New York City. He had taken over the organization when a Mexican gang had gunned down his father in a failed assassination attempt. Frank Sullivan was one of the top organized crime figures in Hell's Kitchen. He was now fighting for his life at NY Presbyterian on the Upper East Side.

I had done well for both father and son. I always made sure to complete any job they gave me without questions. Patrick made it clear that if I ever needed help or wanted my old job back he would be there for me.

I tapped his name from my contacts and he

answered the call after a few rings.

"Hi Patrick. How's your Dad doing?"

"Much better, thanks. He'll be getting out of the hospital in a few weeks. Hey, I have a project for you. I'll pick you up in an hour." Patrick said.

"Sorry, sir, I'm not in New York. Still working some things out, but I've run into a situation overseas. My supplies and cash have been confiscated and I could really use some work to get things going again. Do you have any connections in the UK?" I asked.

"Of course. I'll give Doyle Mulligan a call. Doyle owns an import/export business outside Dublin in a town on the east coast called Wicklow, he could give you some work.

"Thank you, that would be incredibly helpful, sir. A boost like that could help me raise enough money and supplies to get moving to my final destination."

"My dad sent me to stay with him during the summers when I was in my twenties. I learned a lot about the business. Doyle's like an uncle to me so you better behave and treat him well. He'll take good care of you and keep you busy. I'll give him a buzz and tell him about you," Patrick said, and hung up before I got a chance to thank him.

When I left the Indian restaurant, night had settled. I turned right and headed down the street towards the apartment buildings. As I approached I was surprised to see the same group of young hooligans from earlier at the pub. They sat on a set of benches that ran along a walkway in front of the apartment buildings. I knew trouble wasn't far away when they started heckling me.

"Let's fuck him up, Chester," the chubby boy said, with a slight chuckle.

"Don't fuckin' tell me what to do, Barney. Why don't you go mess with him, big shot? He seems pretty harmless maybe you can take him."

Barney strutted toward me with an attitude. He looked over to his mates for reassurance as he came closer. His eyes darted from me to his Chester, as he gathered his courage to continue.

"What-chu got in that bag, old timer?" Barney asked, with bravado.

"Take a look," I said, and threw the bag into his face.

Then I spun and kicked out his feet from behind. Barney went down hard. A big gush of air left his lungs and I followed with a fist to his startled face.

Barney lay sprawled on his back, out cold. His feet twitched, but his breathing was fine. Now I had their attention and Barney's friends stood aghast.

"How'd I do, Barney? Oh sorry. You're speechless," I taunted.

"Alright, alright. Let's see how you do now, old man," Chester said, then he whistled and made a gesture for his boys to move in on me.

Slowly the three of them surrounded me and pulled out knives. They stalled and glanced at each other, I guess trying to figure out who would make the first move.

That's when I swung a roundhouse kick that squarely connected with one of the thug's heads. It bounced sideways and he collapsed to the ground like a rag doll. His knife clattered across the pavement. I turned and faked a punch to another young thug on my right. He flinched and ran off without looking back. That left one knife-wielding thug and he looked scared. Nervously he glanced at Chester.

"Sorry Chester, I gotta go," he shouted, and ran off.

Barney came to, stunned, and wiped at blood that dripped from his nose. He stood on unsteady legs and stumbled towards the buildings.

"So, Chester, just you and me. What's it gonna be?" I asked.

"Yeah, okay, pops. I'm gonna give you something to remember me by." He pulled out a knife.

"What's with you guys and knives?" I asked, but he didn't respond.

Chester was a head taller than me and had the reach advantage, but lacked the experience of a seasoned fighter. He flipped the switchblade from hand to hand like something he'd practiced at home in front of a mirror or seen in a movie. He fainted right and then tried to stab my stomach. I folded over slightly and jumped back. The knife missed by a few inches.

I quickly grabbed my bag up off the ground and used it as a shield. Chester lunged at me, but only stabbed my bag. He tried again and again, but only hit my bag. I swung wide and hit him in the face with bag. The zipper left a small cut on his left cheek. He stumbled backward and touched his cheek, and then looked down to see if it was bleeding.

"No blood yet, pal just a little scratch."

He squinted and gave me a severe look. We stood there and measured each other when a car approached. Chester saw it first and folded his knife and dropped it into his pocket in a flash.

"What seems to be the problem here?" Constable Lawson said, leaning out the car window. When he saw who was involved, he climbed out.

"No trouble, Constable. Chester was just showing me where he lives," I said.

"Is that right? That's doubtful," Constable Lawson said, and straightened his navy jacket.

"Why don't you run home like a good lad, Chester?"

Chester grunted, but stood his ground in protest.

"You'd better leg it, son, before I change my mind and lock you up for the night." He paused briefly, and then smacked his baton into his palm.

"And I mean move it!" he shouted.

He turned to me and saw I was still holding my bag with both hands like a pillow.

"A bit of cat and mouse, aye Mister O'Brien? The only question is who is the cat? Are you playing with these hooligans?"

"No, sir. I was just trying to find a taxi after dinner," I explained.

"We don't need any trouble around here tonight. Are we clear?"

"Crystal clear, sir," I said.

"Alright then. Have a good evening," Constable Lawson said, with a final nod and climbed back into his small car and slammed the door shut. He gunned the engine, put it in gear, and pulled away from the curb.

I called the number on Benny's card and he showed up in less than five minutes with a big grin on his face.

"How's that for service?" Benny said, with pride.

"Truly impressive, Benny."

We drove over to the Central Railway Station on Blechynden Terrace. He didn't say much on the ride over, but wished me a good holiday. I thanked him, then paid and tipped him well.

"Call me up again on your way back. Alright mate?"

"I sure will, Benny. See ya around."

I got out of the cab and walked through a courtyard of grey concrete buildings to the platform. I couldn't fly to Ireland for fear the FBI might have sent my picture to Interpol. Airport security would surely be looking for me. I couldn't take any chances.

The high-speed mega train roared into the station and the conductor blew the horn as the train passed. A cool blast of air whipped at me as the train's brakes let out a squeal. Metal on metal until it stopped with a grinding halt.

I took the train to London, where I slept in the terminal until morning. Then I transferred to another train heading to the Holyhead Ferry Terminal on the west coast. The Welsh countryside was luscious, green, and hilly with small towns and beautiful farmland.

I stood on a long line of chatty tourists with backpacks and cameras waiting for the early ferry to

Ireland. One family I met had traveled from New Jersey. The wife asked me to take a few pictures of them. I guess they thought I was a local, but I didn't say a word just nodded and took the pictures. The parents hugged their children, a cute boy and girl. They had small faces, round cheeks, and giggled with gummy smiles.

A horrible pang of sadness tore at my heart. I had always wanted my own family and kids, but not with my current career. I felt envious of the adorable vacationing family. They had a wealth of happiness I could only dream of as I continued to struggle to get through each day to find a normal life.

I wasn't expecting such a giant ferry to pull into the dock. *Ulysses* was four stories tall and looked like a white floating hotel.

We crossed the channel at high-speed. The mist sprayed my face as I searched the horizon and wondered what fate awaited me in Wicklow. The morning sky changed from a gorgeous cerulean blue to a cloudy gray as we crossed the channel. The waves were choppy as they crashed against the ferry. The ferry itself was completely unaffected by the sea's onslaught and careened onward.

I drifted back into my thoughts and wondered how long the police would hold Yuri and the boys before they'd be released or deported. I watched whitecaps and followed their rhythm as they rolled by.

CHAPTER FOURTEEN

We arrived at the dock in Dublin and I caught a taxi to meet Doyle Mulligan at his office in Wicklow.

"Where to, mate?" the driver asked in a gruff brogue.

I gave him the address and he seemed upset.

"Why would you go there?" he asked, with a scowl.

"I have a business meeting there. Why?"

"Some unsavory characters in those parts, sir, but that's none of my business. Just wanted to let you know is all."

"Thanks for the warning."

He repeated the address and looked at me in the rearview mirror. I nodded, and didn't say another word throughout the ride, but he continued to eye me from his mirror.

When we arrive at Mulligan's, I was surprised to find it really wasn't an office at all, but a charming two-story cottage surrounded by green farmland.

I paid and tipped the driver who appeared extremely nervous, then stepped out into the cool, damp air. The taxi abruptly took off before I could even finish closing the door. The exhaust smoke ruined the air for a few minutes while I took in the rolling green hills and fields.

Doyle Mulligan was an ex-boxer who ran his operation from this farm located about fifty miles from Dublin, but that didn't stop him from getting his hooks into all kinds of activities around the Dublin suburbs. His crews knocked over trucking shipments and collected loans and "protection" payments from small businesses, and he also owned a few tenements and a gym on the outskirts of Dublin.

In downtown Dublin, Mulligan ran several gambling establishments for high-end, no-limit poker. His catering and prostitution businesses worked together to create a great experience for his clientele, rich businessmen and hoodlums with deep pockets.

A stone, waist-high wall separated the cottage from the farm. I stepped through the front gate, which was framed by a high green hedge that led to a cobblestone walkway. It was hard to believe a man that ran a crime organization worked from such a quaint and charming location.

I looked for a doorbell, but only found a large brass knocker to bang on the wooden door. After a couple of loud knocks I heard footsteps approaching from the other side. The door opened slowly and a strikingly gorgeous redhead with shoulder-length wavy hair, alabaster skin, and emerald green eyes took my breath away. She looked like a porcelain doll peeking out from behind the door.

"Yes? Can I help you?" she asked, in a soft voice with an Irish lilt.

I stood there unable to speak or move as I stared into her eyes.

"Are you here to see my father?"

"I… I'm sorry. Yes," I said, fumbling my words.

"I'm Bill. Your father is expecting me." I gave her an awkward toothy smile.

"I'm Anna. Please come in. Dad's in his office on a call."

The inside of the cottage was decorated in an old-world style. Floral patterned wallpaper and small tables with shaded lamps lit up the interior. She led me down a long hallway with brass sconces that added a warm light to old black and white photos of generations of Mulligans.

I followed behind, her my boots thudding dully on the polished wood floor. I watched her curves sway in her white dress as she led me to the office, my eyes glued to her rear end. Anna's shoulders were bare and I ogled her skin until she turned to check on me. Embarrassed, my eyes darted to the floor, and she let out a slight giggle.

She motioned me to a small room outside the office. "Wait here and I'll check if he's ready for you. Please, have a seat."

"Thank you."

If I kept this up Doyle would kill me before I even started working for him.

I sat in the little alcove on one of three ladder-back chairs with patterned seat cushions. Large windows looked out onto a luscious green field behind the cottage. I gazed off into the distance at a tree standing alone. I needed to make some good money and get back on the road quickly. How long would it take me to win Doyle Mulligan's trust? I didn't know, but I'd do my best.

Anna returned after a short while. I immediately stood, my hands folded politely in front of me.

"He'll come and get you shortly. In the meantime, can I get you something to drink?"

"I don't want to trouble you, but some water would be great."

"Alright, I'll be right back."

Anna returned within minutes and placed a glass of iced water on a coaster.

"It was nice meeting you, Bill."

"Likewise. I mean, nice to meet you too, Anna." I was stumbling over my words as she left the room.

I took a sip of the water just as Mulligan popped out of his office.

"Hello, Bill. C'mon in.

He grabbed my hand and shook it with vigor in his steel grip. Pain shot through my palm as I felt my bones grind together.

Doyle Mulligan was in his mid sixties and stood over six feet tall. He had a ruddy complexion, and a full head of hair streaked with white and gray, which he parted to the side. His barrel chest ran straight into his large gut. He wore a medium gray suit with a blue collared button-down dress shirt.

I followed him into a spacious office. Two cushy brown leather chairs faced a large wooden desk scattered with papers and a laptop that sat open. A hefty old balding guy with a bulbous nose and pockmarked face sat in one of the chairs with his feet up on the desk. A cloud of smoke hovered above him as he puffed on a thick cigar. He wore a red polo shirt and blue jeans, and looked like he was on vacation. It was hard to tell who he was, but the gun holster on his hip made it clear that he was much more than a grounds keeper.

An armoire filled with boxing trophies validated Mulligan's passion for boxing. The walls were covered with framed pictures from years past. Most were of young fighters with trophies, and a few event posters that must've had sentimental value. Several more recent color photos showed groups of young kids training wearing emerald green shorts, sleeveless shirts with bright yellow trim, and black boxing gloves. Mulligan and a couple of old trainers stood on either side of the boys with big smiles, like in elementary school class pictures. A few newspaper clippings about Mulligan's big fights from back in the day had been matted and framed with care, and were mounted on the wall directly behind his chair.

Mulligan dropped into a dark brown leather chair behind his desk. He picked up a bottle of Jameson 12 Year Old Irish whiskey and poured an inch into two lowball glasses.

"Please have a seat, Bill. I'd like to introduce a friend of ours. Chief Constable Gerry Alleyn."

"Nice to meet you," I said, and stuck out my hand.

He nodded, but didn't shake my hand. He puffed out another smoke cloud, reached for his whiskey, and took a big gulp. He returned the cigar to his mouth, sat back, and puffed some more. The small room filled up with cigar smoke, but no one cared.

"Bill's a friend of Frankie Sullivan's boy Patrick

over in America, and he's come to work with us for a wee bit. I'm gonna put him to the test with Tommy and the boys at the gym," Mulligan said, and smiled.

"That's a bloody long way to come for some work, lad. What are ye daff or desperate?"

"I've always wanted to come to Ireland. The countryside is so beautiful."

"He looks real green, Doyle. Are you sure the boys won't ruin his delicate sensibilities?"

"He's got quite a reputation, Gerry. I guess we'll have to see if he can hold his own," Mulligan replied.

"Do you know your way around the ring?" the chief asked.

"I've had my share of fights."

"Where? In a school yard?" the chief barked.

"No, in the U.S. Army."

"Oh, a soldier boy. This should be good. Did they train you all proper or kick you out of boot camp?"

"Now, now Gerry, give the lad a break. Let's see what he's got first."

"Alright, we'll see, but I have my doubts. Oh Ireland is so beautiful it is? He might be a bit light."

He took another sip of his whiskey, stood, and pulled up his pants.

"I've got to go Doyle. I'll call your mobile later," he said.

Then walked out, a trail of smoke following him out the door.

"Well, lad, don't mind old Gerry. He's seen lots of hard times over the years. Being a constable isn't a dream job for most men, even if you are the chief. So you like our countryside, aye? Let's take a wee walk up the road and I'll tell you about your new mates."

We stepped outside and walked past the hedges. Mulligan took a few steps past the gate then turned right onto the deserted road in front of his house. He looked back to make sure I followed and continued on. I turned up my collar, surveyed the gray overcast sky, and quickly caught up with a slight limp. The damp weather had aggravated bones that had been broken in the past.

We casually strolled down the gorgeous country road for more than a mile. Our pace was slow and I kept my eyes down on the road and occasionally kicked a random stone. Mulligan remained silent for the most part until I noticed an old tortoise shell comb on the ground and knelt to pick it up.

"No, don't touch that!" he barked, startling me.

"Why?"

"The Banshees. They'll come in the night and steal your soul."

I straightened myself and stepped over the comb without a word. I hurried my paced to keep up with him, but wondered to myself what the Banshees superstition was in Ireland.

The road rolled down a slight hill and curved to the right. We came over the hill to a barn surrounded by a large wired fence with gray stonewalls that divided the animals into different groups. The walls were made out of pilled old stones and looked as if it had been there for hundreds of years. Several fluffy sheep with black faces gathered in the distance eating grass. As we approached the front gate a couple wandered over and called to us. Their desperate bleats for food made me laugh and seemed so foreign to me after living my whole life in New York City.

Mulligan unlocked a gate, pushed it open, and closed it behind us. We continued down a long gravel road that led to an old brown barn. Once inside, he closed the large wooden doors and an intense odor of animal excrement assaulted my senses. On one side were pigpens and on the other chicken coops. We walked straight through to the other side and out the back.

The cool air was a welcome relief from the rancid barn. Mulligan seemed amused by my reaction to the odor in the barn.

"You ever work on a farm, Boyo?" he asked, with a chuckle.

"No, sir. I grew up in New York City."

"Well, lucky for you I have other plans for our business relationship. I want you to come to the boxing gym and meet my boy Tommy. He and his crew could use the help of someone more seasoned with a good head on his shoulders."

"I'll help out wherever I can. What are we doing out here?" I asked.

"I wanted to show you something before we start

working together. It's over here." He pointed to a stone wall off in the distance as we headed over.

We walked through the grass until we reached the wall. Mulligan slapped the top, took a deep breath, and let out a big sigh.

I stepped over to the wall and realized it was a family cemetery. A black, wrought-iron gate defined its solemn borders. At its center was a beautiful statue of woman wrapped in a shawl with her arms held out. Surrounding the statue were fourteen small headstones. Old and worn, they leaned at odd angles from years of rough weather. Some names were unreadable, eroded by time and the elements.

At the far end of the cemetery a group of unmarked graves seemed odd and a chill shook me. A final resting place for the unknown departed. The only marker was a flat slate tile with a neatly cut log mounted on top. Mulligan seemed so solemn I didn't dare ask any questions.

"This is our family's cemetery. My sweet Elizabeth watches over these sad souls and our grazing flock. I lost her to the birth of our youngest son, Tommy. The climate hasn't been kind to her statue or these headstones. The nameless graves are for those who chose not to stay loyal to our family. Let this be a reminder to you. Are we clear, lad?"

He gave me a severe stare and narrowed his eyes.

"Yes, sir," I replied, and stared down at my boots, made damp by the moist grass.

In a flash he grabbed my jacket with both fists and threw me on the ledge of the cemetery wall. He moved so fast that I hardly had time to react. His face took on a wild feral expression. His hot breath blew into my face and his cold gray eyes were inches from mine. A vein popped out on his flushed forehead as his rage flared.

"Are we clear?" Mulligan growled.

He frantically searched my eyes, released me, and stared down at his clenched fists in anguish.

I exhaled loudly not realizing I'd been holding my breath the whole time.

He turned back to face the statue of his wife.

"Tommy is an unpredictable mess. He's become brash and disrespectful with the town folk. You'll look after him until I give you something else to do. Hopefully you can teach him some manners."

"I'll do my best to keep an eye on him. Maybe after we get to know each other he'll accept my counsel."

"I like that. Counsel. He needs a lot of counseling. But, hear my words, Bill. Stay true to my family or I'll put you in the ground with the others."

CHAPTER FIFTEEN

I went back to Mulligan's office to grab my bag and waited for him outside. He pulled out of the garage in a large black BMW 730 sedan. I climbed in and took in the new car aroma of the plush tan leather interior. He drove us into Blackrock on M11, about thirty minutes north.

I remained quiet during the trip and listened to the classical music on the high-end car audio system. I recognized the selection immediately as Vivaldi's "Four Seasons," a piece I loved. The beautiful and somber notes filled the sedan with an odd tranquility I knew was temporary.

I spend most of the time in quiet reflection as I stared out the window. I fidgeted with my jacket zipper and thought back to the conversation with Mulligan at the family cemetery. If he could snap into a full rage during a simple discussion, what would he be like if something went wrong? I needed to keep him happy.

I wondered how long it would take to gather up enough money to buy the arsenal I needed to face Viktor and his brother's crew, but I didn't even know how large their organization was. When this was all done I'd have to contact Yuri. Hopefully his sister would know his whereabouts or how to get in touch with him. Russia was an enormous shadowy land, where I didn't speak the language or know the terrain. I desperately needed his help and hopefully Robert and Garry would be available to add their skills into the mix.

In any case, I needed to stay in Ireland long enough to keep my word to Mulligan and honor the referral from Patrick Sullivan.

I climbed out to the sedan and faced Mulligan's gym. The name engraved over the main entrance, read "Doyle's Fitness Club." Its exterior was modern stucco with large windows that exposed the activities inside. A six-foot black metal fence surrounded the building and parking lot. The added security must've been needed for this neighborhood or maybe just to protect the gym's content from hooligans after closing.

We entered the gym and a familiar odor of leather and sour sweat immediately filled my nostrils. Heavy and speed bags filled up most of the ceiling space, along with fluorescent lights. They surrounded two large boxing rings, which were the main showcase of the gym. Padded mats covered the floors. The inside walls were decorated with event posters, newspaper clippings and framed photographs of members.

In one of the rings, two women in their mid-twenties sparred wearing gloves and headgear, grunting as they slammed each other hard with punches. Sweat dripped from their bodies as they danced around the ring while several men watched. Two older men that looked like coaches shouted to the women to keep gloves up, duck, and move.

I glanced back to notice Doyle shaking hands with practically every person he encountered. Charisma emanated from him and his laugh was contagious. Mulligan's greetings seemed to inspire young fighters throughout the gym.

In the second ring, a solitary young man shadowboxed. He moved around the ring at a furious pace, soaked with sweat and a red flushed face, swinging and ducking. When Doyle approached, he stopped, pulled off his gloves, and climbed through the ropes. A tall, thin young man in his mid-twenties, he had scar tissue on his ears, which made them puffy and hid their true shape. He had a flat nose and a scruffy, unshaven baby face with shocking blue eyes. His brown hair was cut short. He embraced Mulligan, leaving sweat spots all over his gray suit jacket.

"Meet me boy. He's the top fighter in the club. Tommy, this is Bill Conlin from New York, and he's going to be with us for a bit."

"Hi Tommy, nice to meet you," I said, and held out my hand.

"Pleased to me you too," Tommy said.

He shook my hand with the crushing vise grip that seemed to run in the family.

"You got a good grip there."

"Wait a tic, you're a real New Yorker? Wow, I have a ton of questions for you, mate. What part of New

York?"

"Manhattan."

"Brilliant. Let me clean up and we'll have us a proper greeting with a pint."

"Sounds good."

"Tommy will set you up with a place to stay. Okay Tommy?"

"Straight away, Da. He can stay in one of our flats. I'll be right out mate," Tommy said, and walked off to the showers.

"Mind what I told you," Mulligan reminded me.

"Yes, sir. I will."

"Come by the house tomorrow morning around ten for a chat. I've got a project for both of you."

"Sure thing, Mr. Mulligan."

Mulligan gave me a side-glance with a nod, and left. I felt a little out of place and immediately became aware of many eyes on me. The club members didn't stop what they were doing, but their eyes darted my way every few seconds. Maybe I was just paranoid, being an outsider, but I couldn't help but sense something else was going on. I returned their looks with a slight smile and a nod, then sat in a folding chair against a wall and waited for Tommy. Tommy emerged from the locker room with a couple of friends. He wore blue jeans and a gray T-shirt, along with a short black leather jacket and a white baseball cap with a gold symbol that looked like graffiti. His buddies were dressed similarly and together they looked like a New York Hip Hop group.

"Alright Mr. Big Apple, let's go get us a pint."

He didn't introduce me to his buddies, just headed toward the exit. I followed along last, but kept pace and caught up quickly to Tommy.

"Who are your friends? And where can I get a cool hat like you guys?" I asked.

Tommy sneered at me.

"What's that? You fucking wanker?"

He got in my face and his fists immediately clenched by his sides.

"Take it easy, I'm just fucking around," I said, and shrugged.

"I get it. You're one of those funny blokes."

The tension subsided quickly as he playfully

grabbed me in a headlock and pulled me towards the exit. I quickly grabbed my bag as we stumbled into the lot.

CHAPTER SIXTEEN

By the time we got outside, dusk had settled. I reached inside my jacket and dug out a hard-pack of Marlboro Reds. I twisted one into my mouth and then offered a smoke to the boys. Their faces scrunched up in disgust.

"You boys have names?" I asked, and lit up a smoke.

The tip flared bright red with my first hard drag. I blew the smoke out the side of my mouth and we walked down the street.

"Yeah, I'm Needles and this is Broly."

Broly was stocky with a dopey face and a scraggly goatee that he constantly fingered. Needles was lean and tall with sharp pointy features and a pock-marked face. He stood and a head taller than Tommy, but without the muscle mass.

"Hey, Tommy, I'd like to drop off my stuff. Can you show me where I'll be staying?" I asked.

"Okay, but not til we have us a proper meet and greet. Right?" he said, with a big grin.

"Bang on," Broly said, and mimicked Tommy's grin.

"C'mon, mate. My ride is on the next block," Tommy said, and gestured down the street.

"Just let me dump my stuff."

"Fine, it's right up here," he said, and continued walking.

We arrived at an attached three-story tan brick townhouse. Tommy unlocked the door and we entered. The place had an old musty smell and I followed Tommy up the stairs to the third floor. My legs began to burn as we reached the top landing. He walked over to apartment 3C, unlocked two deadbolts and flung the door open.

The living room had a bay window that faced the street. An old worn leather recliner sat next to a beat-up couch with a small TV in front of it. A couple of stained end tables framed the couch. There were empty beer bottles everywhere.

"This way. You can have the room in the back."

Tommy led me down a long narrow corridor and passed a small kitchen in the middle. It seemed claustrophobic without windows and had a sour aroma from a sink filled with dirty dishes. We reached the two doors at the far end of the long hallway and Tommy opened the left bedroom.

"There you go, mate. Just drop your shite here and let's go."

The room was the size of a closet with two red brick walls, a mattress on the floor, and a set of drawers against a plaster wall.

I threw my bag on the bed and Tommy handed me a key.

"You get to share this flat with Needles. He's not the cleanest bloke, but it's just a place to crash. Me and Broly are next door. Now let's get outta here and get us that pint," Tommy said.

A misty rain had started as we stepped out to the street and that drink was starting to sound real good. "Some coffee and bourbon would be nice. This weather's gonna give me a chill," I said, but everyone ignored me.

"Here she is. Ain't she a beaut?" Tommy asked.

He unlocked the doors of a new, bright red Volkswagen GTI. He opened the right door and pulled the seat forward for Broly to get into the back. Needles went around to the left side.

"You get the rear, Captain America, my legs won't fit." Needles folded down the front seat and gestured for me to squeeze in.

"Hurry the fuck up," he blurted, and shot me a nasty glare.

I crawled into the back and was promptly smacked in the knees by the front seat. The impact shot a sharp pain into my legs and I clutched at them with a grunt.

"That's what you get for being so slow," Needles taunted.

"Thanks for caring, Needles. You're a real pal."

"Ha, pal? So fucking American… I love it," Tommy said.

Tommy wasn't a great driver and it was soon clear that passenger comfort was at the bottom of his list. Each time he pressed the clutch and shifted my head jerked back.

"You're gonna give me whiplash, you fuckin' prick!" Broly shouted and punched the back of Tommy's seat.

"Piss off, you fuckin' wanker!" Tommy shouted back to him.

He continued his jerky shifting as we drove up the coast on Route 118, through several small towns, and took a left into Donnybrook on Stillorgan Road, which was also known as M11. It was a clean two-lane motorway that looked newly paved and took us right into the heart of Dublin. I had no idea that Dublin was so modern and hip with bars and stores.

We passed a gorgeous block-sized Victorian building with stone columns at its entrance. I turned to Broly and asked, "What's that?"

"Trinity College. Lots of hot tarts go there."

We finally reached the pub, a place called The Long Hall. Tommy explained that he liked the place because it was so close to Trinity and also the extremely trendy shopping area on Grafton Street, which was apparently a girl magnet.

CHAPTER SEVENTEEN

Tommy drove around until he saw another car pulling out of a spot and he took it. As we walked a few blocks to pub, he boasted about getting a girl for each of us.

"We'll find us a ripe one," Tommy bragged.

"Maybe we'll all get lucky tonight," Broly said.

"Luck's got nothing to do with it, mates. I've got this," Tommy said, holding up a small envelope of white powder.

"What the fuck is that?" I asked.

"Aw, mister prim and proper. Now don't worry, captain. You'll get your dick wet, too," he said, with a malicious giggle.

"I don't need an unconscious date. That's messed up."

"This ain't your fuckin' town," Needles snapped.

We turned the corner onto South Great George's

Street. The pub had a red and white striped awning, which made it stand out from the other businesses on the block.

A bunch of college students were out front smoking and talking.

Inside, the walls were painted red with gold trim. Red and gold carpeting covered the floor, and a dark, old-fashioned wooden bar ran the length of the place.

The pub was completely packed with young people having a great time and the noise level was deafening. I felt old and out of place in this crowd where the average age seemed to be about twenty-one, like I was someone's older brother. Some of the younger faces looked as if they were barely old enough to drive let alone drink.

Tommy checked out the women with predator's eyes, looking for a stray victim to hunt. Broly and Needles ordered shots of whiskey and beers at the bar as Tommy headed over to a group of four girls way back near the restrooms.

He seemed genuinely charming and appeared to have won them over fairly quickly with his friendly banter. He was throwing punches in the air, apparently boasting about his boxing abilities. I couldn't understand his wanting to drug someone. He could easily have gotten a date with one of these girls without pulling any tricks. It had to be some kind of power trip. What a prick.

The girls looked safe in numbers for the time being so I squeezed my way over to the bar and ordered a Guinness and bourbon from a cute blonde bartender, but got a Jameson instead.

I shrugged it off and made my way through the crowd back to my spot where I gulped the shot of Irish whiskey and chased it down with the cool Guinness as I continued to keep an eye on Tommy. He was quite slick, putting on a good show of pretending to be listening attentively to them.

When I turned back to the bar, I was surprised to find a pale-faced Goth girl looking me up and down with striking blue-green eyes.

Black was definitely the theme with her long, raven-black hair, thick eyeliner, and black nail polish. She wore a leather biker jacket over a short flared lace dress with mesh stockings and combat boots. Her dress was tied up the front, with a hint of a red lace bra that peeked out showing off her ample cleavage. I couldn't help but stare at her breasts as they rose with each breath. She wore a couple of strands of dark beads around her neck, which she played with as she stared at me. Aside from the bra, the only color she wore was a shock of red lipstick.

Her beauty struck me hard. She was definitely pretty under all that makeup. I wanted to know her. I took a deep sip of the black Guinness and downed the rest of the Jameson.

I gave her a thin smile, but she didn't return it, only narrowed her eyes and stuck out her tongue like a little kid. I got a glimpse of a silver ball pierced through her tongue and laughed. I took another big swig of the cool stout and moved toward her. Our eyes met and I panicked for something clever to say.

"Did that hurt?"

"Really? Is that the best you can do?"

"Excuse me?" I said.

"You heard me."

"Okay, sorry, I'll leave you alone. I didn't mean to bother you."

"Wait a tic, your voice sounds funny. I mean your accent."

"So does yours."

"No, really. Where are you from?" she asked, suddenly intrigued.

"New York."

"New York?" she said, and mimicked my accent. "You sound like someone from one of those American gangster movies."

"So, are you gonna tell me your name?"

"I don't think so."

I looked around, trying to get a handle on the conversation, and then our eyes met again. There was definitely something sexy about her.

I took another swig of my beer and looked down at my shoes. *Say something clever,* I thought, but the best I could come up with was, "What do you do in this town?"

She widened her eyes and cocked her head.

"So, you're interested in what I do? I go to school."

"You mean the one with the big columns? A few blocks from here?" I asked.

"No, that guess was shite. There's only like a dozen schools in Dublin."

"I guess you don't really look like a university type."

"Really? And what do I look like?"

"Maybe a creative or musical type."

"That's good, you're getting warmer. I go to the National College of Art and Design."

"So, you're an art student. What's your major?"

"Does this usually work on other girls?"

"I don't know. I'm not much of a talker."

I glanced back over at Tommy still chatting up the table of girls. Two got up and walked away.

"What's so interesting about that bloke over there? Is he your lover?"

"What? No. You could say I'm his big brother and just keeping an eye on him so he doesn't get into trouble. I'm Bill, by the way. And you are?"

"Nice try, Brother Bill. I don't think so, besides you look too old for this place."

"Wow, you're tough. I like that."

This time she gave me a smile and a giggle. "You do?"

"Are all your friends from that art school?" I asked.

"Art students don't have much money, so they stay in a lot. It's boring."

The rest of the girls got up and left Tommy's table. He looked around, and then headed over to us.

"Where'd all your friends go?" I asked, as he approached.

"They've got fucking school work to do or some shite. At least that's what they said." He turned to her. "Who's this vampire?"

"Piss off," the Goth-girl hissed.

"This is the countess of Dublin," I said, hoping to lighten things up a little.

"Would you like a drink… um…?" I stalled.

"Janette. And yes, I'll have an Amaretto Sour."

"You got it, Tommy?"

"Nah, I'm good mate."

I weaved my way through the crowd of partying students and reached the bar. I ordered an Amaretto

Sour for Janette and another bourbon for me. I'd asked for Knob Creek, but they gave me Marker's Mark. At least this time I'd gotten bourbon, so things were looking up.

I spotted the other guys at the opposite end of the bar. Needles did a shot of whiskey, then chased it with his beer and shouted something to Broly. It must've been hilarious, since both laughed so hard. They abruptly stopped and turned to Tommy's direction. Tommy was unsuccessfully trying to put the moves on Janette. He whispered in her ear and tried to kiss her neck, but she promptly shoved him away. Tommy was such a dickhead I could barely stand him. Mulligan warned me that he needed guidance and he was spot on.

I returned and handed Janette her Amaretto Sour.

"I gotta go," she said, repulsed, though with a nervous smile. "Your friend's a pig."

"Stop putting the move on my girl," I chided Tommy, and gave Janette a wink.

He leaned over and whispered. "She'll do fine, mate. Make sure she finishes that drink. Once she's

out we'll run a train on her all night back at my flat."
Tommy's breath was hot in my ear. I felt utterly
disgusted and pulled away.

He put his arm behind Janette and poured the
white power into her drink. She shoved him away
again, with the same irritated expression.

"This one's feisty. How fun."

"I'm leaving," she said. "You can keep your drink
and your gross friend."

"Hold on girl, wait a sec," I said, and gave Tommy
a nasty look.

"I get it. I'll leave you two alone," Tommy said, and
confidently strutted over to Needles and Broly at the
bar.

"I hate jock pricks like him. Keep that fucker away
from me," she said.

"He's not my friend. I just work with his father. I'm
sorry he's a little aggressive. I guess he's taken too
many punches to the head."

I glanced over at the bar, the boys laughed and
watched us with anticipation. Tommy nodded
encouragement for me to continue with his plan. He

made a gesture of pretending to drink from a glass.

I leaned in and whispered, "You wanna get out of here? There's gotta be a better place to get to know each other."

"Sure, just let me finish this," she said, and reached for the drink.

Time slowed as I watched her bring the glass up to her parted lips. I only had seconds to act. I knocked the glass out of her hand and rushed in with a hard kiss on her mouth.

The glass bounced on the floor, the ice clinking as the noxious concoction spilled onto the carpet.

I thought she was going to smack me, but to my surprise she squeezed me in a tight embrace. I became immediately aroused by her scent. Powdery undertones with hints of citrus and something clean and fresh that I couldn't identify, but thought it might be ginger.

"Well, well. That was a nice surprise. I didn't think you had it in you."

Janette traced her fingers over her soft red lips, as she seemed to drift some place deep in her mind.

"Do I have lipstick on my face?" I asked.

"What? A little." She smirked as she wiped her red lipstick off my mouth.

I glanced over at the bar to spy Tommy, clearly infuriated with a flushed face and clenched fists. I'd spoiled his plan, which threw him into a full on tantrum. Tommy pounded the bar and shoved Broly against the wall in frustration as they argued about what had just happened.

"We'd better get going," I said, and pulled Janette to the door.

CHAPTER EIGHTEEN

We stepped out into the cool night air. The streetlights glared in the misty evening and reflected in her eyes.

"Which way?" I asked.

"This way," she said, and pulled me along. We ran north toward the River Liffey and stumbled along, laughing like kids the whole way to her flat. We made a left on Lord Edward Street and headed west until it turned into Thomas Street.

"This is my place, right here on the left," Janette said when we stopped in front of a three-story red brick building.

"Come up for a bit and I'll show you my stuff. I mean my art."

"I just wanted to get you home," I said, hesitating.

I was worried for her safety. Trouble was never far off with my new line of work.

"Don't worry I won't bite. Much," she joked.

"Do you have roommates?" I asked.

"Nah, my parents set me up me here cause I didn't want to be in the dorms. I like the solitude. Keeps my creative juices flowing."

She unlocked the door and pulled me into a dimly lit, black-and-white tiled corridor. A couple sconces lit the way. No garbage, odd odors, or junk cluttered up the hallway like my old nasty place in New York.

"It's apartment three at the end of the hall," she said, and pulled me by my hand.

Our boots echoed loudly as we made our way down the quiet hallway. I leaned on the wall and watched as she inserted keys into two deadbolts then opened the door.

A strong scent of turpentine and paint immediately hit me, strong but not offensive.

"Sorry about the mess. I paint every day and it takes a while for the oils to dry."

In the living room, several small tables were loaded with dozens of jars that contained brushes and a wide range of colorful paints. Several finished paintings were stacked around the edge of the room. I spotted a large, loose canvas stapled to the wall, a painting of a Raggedy Ann doll hanging from a noose. I stepped in for a closer look, onto a tarp that protected the floor.

"This is pretty gruesome, but I guess it goes with your whole black theme."

"What black theme?" she asked.

"Umm, I just thought… forget it," I replied.

I peered around the room, taking in her art studio. I'd never met an artist before, and I was intrigued.

"Want a drink?" she asked, and headed toward the kitchen. "All I have is vodka and beer."

"A beer would be great," I said, and watched her curved bottom as she bent over to grab the beer from the back of the refrigerator.

She turned her head and caught me watching her rear. She smiled and handed me a cold brown bottle with a familiar label.

"Bud?

"Oh, you didn't think we like American beer?"

"No, it's just that I was expecting something local."

"Well, too bad. Let's toast."

"What should we toast to?

"To new friends. Sláinte," she said. She clinked her bottle into mine and took a deep swig.

"What's that mean?"

"To your health. It's like an Irish version of cheers."

"Say it again?"

"Sláinte."

"I like that." I tried to repeat it, but completely butchered the pronunciation. She let out a big laugh and punched me in the chest.

I moved in slowly to kiss her mouth. Her lips were soft, warm, and wet. She parted her lips and our tongues slowly chased each other for a brief moment.

I put the bottle on the counter. I held her tight and moved my hands down her back to cup her bottom as I pulled our bodies together. I released her and she gasped softly. I didn't realize I'd been holding my breath too and let it out. She giggled, took my hand, and led me through the living room to her bedroom, which was nothing like the art studio at the center of her apartment. It was clean, had no art supplies, with an armoire, a TV, a beautiful wooden bed frame and a plush comforter. She dragged me down on the bed and rolled on top of me.

We kissed breathlessly for a long while, until we worked ourselves into a passionate frenzy. Her breath and tongue were hot in my ear as she rubbed my crotch. I slid my hand under her dress and felt her moist heat. We ripped off our clothes at a crazy pace, lips locked on each other.

Her scent drove me wild, sweet and spicy with a fresh soapy aroma. I kissed my way down to her neck to her hard nipples and soft warm stomach.

Our bodies merged with a hot passion that was nothing short of spectacular. When Janette came, I joined her in a shuttering explosion and a warm release. It left me completely spent and relaxed. A quiet drowsiness descended as I pulled the comforter over my shoulders and drifted into a welcoming slumber.

The next morning, bright light streamed in through an opening in the curtained windows. The aroma of fresh coffee and cooked bacon filled the flat as I lay in bed and listened to the sounds of plates and flatware being pulled from the drawers and cabinets. I took it all in. It satisfied a void deep in my heart. Janette was someone completely unexpected and I felt oddly content.

After a while my phone alarm went off, which was a reminder of my meeting with Doyle Mulligan. I headed into the kitchen where I found Janette wearing my shirt with nothing under it. She looked for something in the refrigerator and I stood transfixed by her beauty. She turned with a bashful smile and placed a jar of strawberry jam on the counter front of me.

"Good morning," I said.

"Hi, you. Sleep well?" she asked, and kissed me full on the mouth.

I sat on a stool by a Formica countertop with a cut through that opened into the kitchen. Janette placed two steaming plates of scrambled eggs, bacon, and toast on the counter.

"How do you like your coffee?" Janette asked.

She reached for two mugs from the top of the cabinets over the sink. I watched her go up on her toes, and ogled her bare athletic legs.

"Cream, no sugar. You look different today. I mean, good without your makeup."

"Still scoring points, aye?" she said, and paused to glare at me before pouring coffee into my mug.

"No really. I mean it," I said, and took a bite of the bacon.

"Close your mouth. You're too noisy."

"Sorry," I said, and pressed my lips together.

I drifted off lost in thoughts about my meeting. The morning with Janette was so nice and normal. I wished I could stay, but with Mulligan being a local crime kingpin my first project had to be dangerous. I just hoped it wasn't a hit.

"You still with us?" Her voice brought me back to the moment.

"I have to get going. I've got business in Wicklow. I want to see you again, if that's alright?"

"Really? Well, I'm very busy so I'm not sure that's possible."

"Okay, I see," I said, dejected.

She smirked at me. "I was only joking. C'mon, of

course I want to see you."

We finished up breakfast and I gave her my number. She grabbed her phone and immediately sent me a text message of a smiley face.

"Call me whenever you want to get together again," she said.

"I'm gonna need that shirt back."

She scurried into the bedroom. A minute later, she came out in another t-shirt and handed me mine.

"Good luck with your meeting and call my mobile later," Janette said, and gave a quick smack to my bottom as she walked me to the door. Before I left, I kissed her. She bit my bottom lip gently and held it for a second. I looked into her bright blue-green eyes as I pulled away. Something stirred inside me. I wanted to kiss her more, but had to leave. I left without looking back, a pang of sadness filled my mind. Maybe things would be normal once I'd sorted out my loose ends, but doubted it.

I walked outside into the cool, damp air and headed back towards the pub, hoping to find a taxi. I passed The Long Hall and waved down a taxi that just dropped off a cute old couple.

I climbed in and asked the driver to take me to Tommy's address in Blackrock. When we arrived, I spotted my bag, abandoned in the street like garbage.

I guess I'll need a new place to stay, I thought to myself.

"Can you wait?" I asked the driver. "I just want to get something and then I have another stop."

"Alright," he said.

I stepped out, picked up my bag, and got back in the taxi. "I'm going to Wicklow," I said, and gave him the address.

We drove for about forty-five minutes until we arrived at Mulligan's cottage. I noticed Tommy's red GTI. I could only image what he'd told his dad after I ditched him and his crew.

I got out of the cab and took the hard pack from inside my jacket pocket. I lit up a cig. I had no way of knowing what kind of bullshit they were going to put me through before trusting me. I knew Tommy wasn't going to trust me. Especially after I ditched him and ran off with Janette. I didn't really care. I'd dealt with his kind before.

CHAPTER NINETEEN

I rang the doorbell. Moments later, I was greeted by Tommy's face, filled with hate and disgust. "You've got a lot of explaining to do, you fucking cunt," Tommy barked. He narrowed his eyes and stepped back behind the door to let me in.

"I do? Let's see what Da says about you gang-raping college students. He might not care, but then again he does have a daughter. Right, mate?" I asked.

"You try it and I'll gut you right in front of him." He eyed me with pure disdain.

"Let's roll the dice and see," I said, with a slight smirk. "Go ahead. Do what you got to do."

I walked past him and into the house.

"Wait here and I'll get you when we're ready." Tommy said, and walked to Mulligan's office.

I sat on a couch with my hands folded in front of me wondering what tale Tommy was crafting. Anna came out of the kitchen and greeted me with a smile.

"Hi Bill, nice to see you. Is everything alright?"

"Yes, just a little nervous. I'm meeting with your dad and brother."

"I'm sure it will be fine. Would you like a spot of tea while you wait?"

"I don't want to be any trouble," I said, struck again by her red wavy hair and striking emerald green eyes.

"No trouble at all. Come sit."

I followed her and sat at a small round table. There was a faint scent of breakfast tea in the air. Anna placed a cup and saucer in front of me and slowly poured the piping hot tea. I looked up and our eyes met, but I glance away embarrassed by what could be a fatal attraction.

"Thank you."

"How do you like your tea? Milk and sugar or honey?" she asked.

"Milk and sugar is fine."

"Here you go." She placed the milk and sugar on the table.

"So Anna, are you in the family business as well?" I asked, and watched the swirling color change as I poured.

"I teach kindergarten part time. I just love those bright innocent little faces so filled with life. They ask the oddest questions. I can't wait to have my own precious family," she beamed.

"I've thought about a family too, but my travels make it difficult," I admitted.

"Thought about what? A family? Yeah, if you live long enough." Tommy interrupted.

"Oh, stop it Tommy. You're so coarse," Anna responded, appalled.

"Don't go near her again," Tommy barked.

"Thanks for the lovely chat, Anna. Have a nice day," I said, and took a last sip.

"I said move it," Tommy demanded.

"Tommy, don't be rude to our guest," Anna said.

"Yeah, don't be so rude," I said, and stood to face him.

"Let's go." Tommy sneered and walked out towards Mulligan's office.

When I entered the room Broly and Needles sat in the leather chairs. Doyle sat behind his large dark wooden desk. Tommy pushed me in and closed the door.

"It seems we have a wee issue here, Bill." Mulligan spoke in an impatient tone. "Your new mates told me how you deserted them and moved out of the flat. I thought we were all clear on your role here, boyo. What's all this about?"

"It's the opposite, sir. I totally appreciate you taking me in and as you know I desperately need your support. Tommy and I had a little misunderstanding on how young ladies should be treated. I tried to show him the proper way of being a gentleman, but he wasn't interested. I thought it would be for the best if I moved on."

"I see," he said, and then abruptly stood.

"Again Tommy?"

"What?" Tommy said, panic in his voice.

"Was I not clear about tricking young girls?" Mulligan shook with rage as he yelled at his son.

"No, Da, I di-didn't do anything," Tommy stuttered, and took a step back against the closed door.

"Again?" A huge vein appeared on his reddening

forehead as he slammed his fist on the desk. We all flinched from the outburst.

"For God's stakes, boy, you have a sister. I know exactly what you're up to. Chief Gerry told me yesterday there had been reports of a boxer type assaulting girls in the area. You've brought shame on our house again and I won't have it. You hear me, boy? I won't have it."

"No, I di-din't do that, Da."

"Eugene, Bret, I'm surprised at the both of you, too. I take you boys in and this is the thanks I get? Shame on the lot of you."

He gazed out the window for a few beats, deep in thought, and then turned back to face us.

"I hoped Bill would teach you boys something about being a man. He's our guest and my old friends in America sent him to help us. Now get your arses up and go clean out the barn."

No one moved. Their eyes darted from to each other, too afraid to look directly at Mulligan. Tommy's attention was focused on his shoes.

"Now!" Mulligan roared.

Needles and Broly shot out of their chairs and stood straight up with terror in their eyes.

"C'mon, Da, really?"

"I had a nice job set up for you, but clearly you're still children and will be treated as such. Now get out of my sight and go clean that shite out of the barn." They shuffled out of the office and tried to avoid eye contact with me.

The thought of that vile barn odor still haunted me from the other day as I turned to follow them.

"Hold on, Bill," he said.

"Yes sir?" I asked.

"I was hoping you could teach my boy some manners, but he's a hot mess. No more babysitting for you. I spoke with Patty Sullivan early this morn, and he told me the crazy story about what you've done for his family. Well done. I had forgotten you were a military man."

He slapped me on the back.

"I have some pressing business of my own that needs sorting. My ignorant son's manners... Well, I'll have to deal with that myself. You're no babysitter," he said. "I've turned my boy into a great boxer and a dangerous spoiled brat." Mulligan paused and scratched at his unshaven chin. "Enough about him for now. In any case, I'm a partner in an import-export business up north. Some young hooligans are interfering with shipments and bothering my manager. You're gonna go over there and set things straight. After all, that is what you do. Right, Bill?"

"Yes sir."

"Yes sir? I like that. Patrick told me about those Russian dogs and what they did to you. It's a dirty shame. Take care of this and I'll get you on your way. Now let's go over to the garage. I can't have my man taking taxis all about Ireland."

He led me into the hallway. "Let's go," he said. I followed him down the corridor, to the garage door. As he opened the door, a strong scent of cars, metal, and motor oil filled my nose. One side of the garage was empty except for a few oil stains. On the other side sat Tommy's new red Volkswagen GTI.

"Here you go lad," Mulligan said, and handed me the keys. "Don't worry about Tommy. He's gonna move home for a while so I can work on his manners. His poor deceased mother would never forgive me if I didn't beat him into being a... What did you say? Oh yeah, 'a proper gentleman.'"

Mulligan turned to a worktable with a set of metal drawers. He pulled open the bottom drawer and took out small silver metal case. The sound of his footsteps echoed loudly as he came towards me in the quiet garage.

"Go see Sean. Here's his card. He's a good bloke and he'll tell you what needs doing. Go set those fuckers straight." Mulligan handed me the case.

Then, without another word, he pressed a button on the wall. A motor roared to life as the door lifted and daylight flowed into the garage.

I stepped on the clutch, started the engine, and shifted into reverse. The engine growled as I backed out of the driveway. The garage door slammed shut as I shifted into first gear and drove to the gate.

Before leaving I looked down at the card. It read: *Black Water Imports, Sean Blake, Manager.* The address was in West Belfast. After I added Sean's contact information in my phone, I grabbed the silver case next to me and opened it. A Beretta 9mm with two extra magazines lay under a wad of cash.

CHAPTER TWENTY

I shook my head. *Babysitting Tommy was probably safer,* I thought to myself and closed the case. I entered the address Mulligan gave me into the map app on my phone.

Black Water Imports was about two hours north of Wicklow. That would give me plenty of time to reflect on my current situation.

As soon as I got on the M11, I called Blake to make sure he was available and put the phone on "speaker" mode. He picked up after three rings.

"Yeah," a rough voice answered.

"Sean? Sean Blake?" I asked.

"Yeah, who's this? I'm busy, make it quick."

"This is Bill," I said, and waited for some recognition, but got none.

"So?"

"Bill Conlin. I work with Doyle Mulligan. I'm coming to help you with your deliveries."

"Just come on in when you get here," he barked, and ended the call.

"Great, another new friend," I said aloud, and sighed.

I arrived to find a neighborhood that was as gray as the overcast sky. A cold rain pelted me as I climbed out of the car and ran to the warehouse. The building looked abandoned, with the front windows boarded up and the rest covered in soot. I rubbed at a window with the side of my fist, but still couldn't see in. I pushed at the door, which was unlocked. The door creaked loudly, and cut through the silence with an eerie echo that rose up through the rafters of the dilapidated warehouse.

"Hello, anyone in there? Hello?" No one responded.

The warehouse was completely empty and dead. I walked towards the back and found racks of wooden crates, but not a single employee. The damp, musty odor of dust and mold made me cough, but I cleared my throat and continued on in the dim light.

"Hello, Mr. Blake. Anyone here?"

Did anyone work here? Had something happened to Mr. Blake?

On the hollowed-out third floor were large windows and a metal walkway with railing that ran the length of the building. The dirty panes let dim rays of light penetrate, which gave the warehouse a dark, smoky atmosphere.

Gradually my eyes adjusted to the darkness and I was able to find a path through the crates. I weaved my way towards the back office, my boots echoing with each step.

I came to a dark green door with a sign that read "Office." On either side of the door were thick, frosted windows with wired mesh between the panes. I tried the door handle, but it was locked.

I was about to knock when I felt something cold pressed hard into the back of my neck.

"Hey, easy there. I'm here to meet with Sean Blake," I said.

"Make a move and I'll cut ya down," a scratchy voice whispered.

"Alright, I don't want any trouble. Take it easy," I

said, with both hands in the air. "Doyle Mulligan sent me."

"I told you not to fucking move. You're makin' a lot of noise in here. What do you want?"

"I called a couple of hours ago. Bill Conlin. I'm here to help get your shipments moving again."

"Oh... ya are? Put your hands down and turn around. Let me have a look at ya."

I slowly dropped my hands, turned, and stepped back against the door.

A tiny, hunched over old man with a weather-beaten face stood before me. He held a large caliber handgun a few inches from my face. The gun looked as big as his head, but I was sure he could still blow my head clean off if I upset him.

Sean Blake was in his late seventies or older and he couldn't lift his head high enough to look me straight in the eye. He tilted his head to the side and peered at me through white bangs that hung over his eyes.

He struggled to lift his head up and started to quiver with the effort, but he remained bent over, with the gun still pointed at my face.

"What the hell are you looking at?" he snapped, now seeming more scared than angry.

"Could you please stop pointing that hand canon at me?"

"You're not in charge here, boyo. So keep ya face shut 'til I ask ya something. Now get the fuck out of the way."

Blake waved his gun and indicated where he wanted me to stand. He shuffled to the office door, unlocked it, and turned to face me.

"Wait here," he said, and stepped inside, where he began ruffling through papers. His voice was low, but I could hear him talking to someone.

"Alright, Doyle, I hear ya. He can? Let him take the next truck over to Blanchardtown? For fucks sake... We're gonna lose another one. Yeah, I'll tell him."

After a few minutes of silence he came out with papers and a set of keys. He pushed the keys and papers into my hand.

"Here, take this. The truck is out back. This way."

I followed him out the backdoor to a loading dock. The truck had a dark green cab and a plain gray metal trailer with no logo or branding of any kind, and was backed up to the loading dock.

"Okay lad, here's the deal. You're heading to Blanchardtown to delivery this shipment to Morris over at Crack Motors. It's a small shop off of Navan Road, northwest of Dublin. Now here's the big kicker, you're not gonna make it." He scanned my face, I guess waiting for a reaction.

"Why's that?"

"Cause the Gallagher brothers will hunt you down and steal that truck before you get to Morris. You'll see. They've hijacked every one of our shipments for months."

CHAPTER TWENTY-ONE

I jumped down from the loading dock. The rain started coming down heavy in sheets and soaked my head and shoulders in seconds. A few drops managed to splash the back of my neck and I shivered. I climbed into the truck and started it up. I pulled around front and retrieved the gun case from the Volkswagen. I snapped a magazine into the Beretta 9mm, and slid back the mechanism chambering a round. I put the safety on and placed the gun in the door compartment. I tapped the auto shop's address into my phone.

After about an hour of driving I started feeling drowsy. I shook myself awake as I cruised by the small towns that bordered the motorway. I kept my speed in check; getting pulled over would have been a disaster. I changed lanes to pass a slow-moving vehicle when I suddenly noticed a red truck coming up fast behind me. I changed lanes again so they could pass me, but they mirrored my actions. The red truck sped up and slammed into me with a loud crack of metal on metal. My truck lurched forward with a shudder and I swerved to keep on the road.

I pressed the accelerator down hard. The engine roared its complaint. The old truck just wasn't fast enough to outrun these hijackers. They rammed me again and my head jerked back and bounced off the seat. I slammed down hard again on the pedal while the speedometer slowly surged to 130kph.

As I raced to get away another red truck pulled out from the shoulder and tried to cut me off, but I veered right and quickly passed them. The first truck rear-ended me again. The grinding force almost pushed me off the road until I regained control. It was clear they knew my route well and were set on stopping me.

"Alright, let's do this," I said aloud.

I hit the gas and collided with the truck in front of me. The impact forced my head forward and it hit the steering wheel. A spike of pain shot through my brain, and spots appeared in my vision. The truck swerved back and forth, but didn't tip over. I got alongside the red truck, then twisted the wheel hard to the left. I smashed into their rear wheel with a loud thud. The impact knocked their truck off balance. It spun out of control and skidded sideways off the shoulder, hit some debris, then caught air and careened into a ditch. It flipped over and over, dirt, grass, and metal chunks exploding in every direction. The truck abruptly crashed and came to a fiery dead stop. I glanced in my side mirror and watched the smoking heap fade into the distance as I raced down the motorway with the other hijackers in hot pursuit.

Bullets suddenly ricocheted inside the cab and shattered the passenger window. A thug leaned out the window and unloaded an AK-47 assault rifle into my truck; it brought back memories of being under fire in Afghanistan. Time froze for a flash as I drifted back to a patrol with my unit. We were loaded down with gear and searching for insurgents that had been reported lurking in a town outside Ghazni Province. It should've been routine, but nothing was predicable over there. An explosion went off up the line and smoke reduced visibility and automatic weapons fire erupted around us. Next to me a wall exploded as AK-47 gunfire ripped into the brick wall above my head. Terrified, I dropped to the ground as chunks of brick, cement and dust rained down.

The side mirror blew apart with a loud crack and shattered glass tapped against my window, violently startling me out of my past. I turned the steering wheel left and right, in a desperate attempt to weave away from their vicious barrage.

I'll be finished if they catch one of my tires, I thought.

I gunned the engine and swerved off onto an exit ramp at the last second. My truck tipped sideways and almost flipped before righting itself.

I gained control and pressed the accelerator to the floor as the old truck roared and hurtled forward at full speed. Small towns whizzed by as I continued south, with the bandits gaining ground. I passed an intersection and had a thought and jammed on the brakes. The truck came to a screeching halt and I jumped an embankment, then took a sharp turn off the main road.

My pursuers missed the intersection, skidding past,

and turned sharply to catch up again. This was my break. I made a quick U-turn and headed straight for the oncoming hijackers. The thug with the AK-47 popped out again and fired off another volley of bullets that pinged off the truck's hood. I ducked down as the front windscreen fractured.

The gunner sneered as I aimed the truck at his side. The trucks collided with an earth-shaking crash and both sputtered in opposite directions before coming to a dead stop. Then everything went black.

I awoke to find my windshield completely shattered as smoke filled the cab from the damaged engine. The hood was bent up at an odd angle. I touched my dripping face and my hand came away wet with blood. Panicking, I grabbed the case off the floor, but the gun wasn't there. I quickly remembered that I had placed it in the driver's door compartment, and pulled it out.

I stumbled onto the pavement, as people emerged shocked by the accident. The backend of the other truck jutted out of a storefront. Glass, metal, and wood littered the street. The goon with the AK-47 lay on the ground by the open passenger door. As he lunged weakly for the rifle, I shot him once in the face. Blood sprayed from his mouth and he collapsed dead. A woman screamed horrified at the sound of gunfire. Frightened townsfolk ducked back into their houses.

I stood frozen and started to feel faint. The driver fell out of the truck a few feet in front of me. His face was covered in blood from a gash on his forehead. I moved in closer and felt sick again, but tried to push it away. I fought a wave of dizziness and struggled to keep my focus

I took a deep breath and stared up at an overcast sky with the Berretta 9mm still in my hand. I instantly checked my surroundings, but no one approached.

The driver lay outside the truck door, unconscious, but alive. His chest rose and fell in short quick breaths. Blood, red and shiny, oozed from the cut over his eye. I nudged him with my foot and he groaned back to consciousness with his hands held up.

"Don't… shoot."

"You wanna end up like him?" I asked, and pointed to his dead partner.

He glared at me through the eye that wasn't damaged and hacked up a glob of bloody phlegm, which he spit it at my feet. He stood, raising his hands in the air. He took a few steps back and collapsed onto the pavement with a loud grunt.

"Where is the last shipment that you fuckers stole?" I asked, through gritted teeth.

When there was no response I pressed the pistol into his temple.

"I don't know," he winced.

I pushed the gun harder against the side of his head, and then slid the mechanism back, which seemed to get his full attention.

"I'm gonna count to three. You don't have to die, but I'll shoot you if you don't tell me something," I said, and took a deep breath.

"One. Two..."

"Alright, alright. Don't shoot. I'll tell. Pleeease," he begged, and squeezed his eyes tight in anticipation.

"Let's hear it."

"There's a town called Swords, northeast of here. The Gallaghers own a company there, Walker's

Property Management. The last haul is all there and it's in the warehouse waiting to be shipped."

"These Gallagher boys have names?" I asked.

"Yeah. Paul is the boss and his younger brother's Terry, but he is just plain mean and crazy. Will ya let me go now?"

A single tear rolled down his face and streaked his blood-coated cheek. I felt horrible shooting an unarmed man, but I needed to stay ice cold. He would've stood back and watched as his associate murdered me. Another wave of dizzy nausea came on. I shook my head, swallowed down the bile, and clenched my teeth.

"I'm sorry," I said, and put my finger on the trigger.

Just pull the trigger, I thought, but I couldn't do it.

I looked at his face and stopped. I couldn't shoot a defenseless man that wasn't trying to kill me. This went against every part of my being. Even if I was a criminal now I didn't want to be a ruthless monster and struggled to keep some small part of my old self.

I stared at him for a few seconds, the tear still wet on his face. I blinked slowly mulling it over, took in a deep breath and sighed.

"Fine, you can go. Go on, get the hell out of here before I change my mind," I barked.

Then before I knew what was happening, footsteps came up fast behind me. I swung around in time to see the butt of a gun smash into my face. I collapsed, unconscious.

I awoke with a splitting headache, not sure how much time had passed. The injured thug was gone, and distant sirens signaled that my time was up.

"I fucking hate this work," I growled aloud as I righted myself.

Why the fuck am I doing this? I thought, but of course I knew why and was completely repulsed by what I'd become.

I walked over to my damaged truck. Smoke, oil, and anti-freeze leaked from the damaged front grill. The radiator had been badly damaged in the crash. Liquid pooled on the ground in a swirl of bright green and black, with a rainbow slick that floated on the surface. The hood was bent up and the bumper pushed under the wheel well.

The bumper had been pushed against the left tire, which would probably stop me from getting too far if I could get the engine started again.

People started coming out to see what had happened. A woman screamed in shock from the dead man that lay in the street. I had no doubt whether the Garda were called, but didn't hear any sirens yet.

I climbed into the cab and tried to close the door, but it was warped out of shape and wouldn't fully close. I turned the key in the ignition. It clicked a few times. It stuttered and knocked a few times before it went dead.

"Fuck, c'mon you bastard!" I yelled, and slammed my fist on the steering wheel.

A pain shot through my head like a white-hot dagger. I swallowed and turned the key again. This time it made a high-pitched whine and the engine jumped to life.

I wasn't sure how far I was going to get with all the fluid dripping from the radiator, but I put it in gear and hit the gas. I was relieved when the truck moved, though no matter how hard I pressed the accelerator, my top speed stayed at 20kph.

I reached into my pocket, took out my phone, and mapped my location. The auto shop was five miles east of my current location. I needed to stay off major roads. The Gallaghers and the Garda would certainly be on the hunt for me.

A wave of dizziness washed over me again and I struggled to keep conscious. I fought off the wooziness, ready to pull over to the shoulder when I saw the auto shop. I pulled the truck into a large open repair bay and someone closed the garage door behind me.

I rested my head on the steering wheel and tried to stay still for a brief moment. A sharp pain ripped through my head and the world spun for a moment behind my eyelids. I squeezed my eyes tight and blinked hard not wanting to black out.

I'm not sure how long I sat there, but someone shook my shoulder.

"Hey mate, are you alright there? You really fucked up this truck."

I opened my eyes to find a man in his thirties with

short, dark hair. His hands and blue work clothes were stained with black grease.

"Yeah, I had to use the truck to stop them. Ugh, my head," I said, and cringed.

"I'm Morris. You should lie down until we get a doctor. Sean is on his way over. I told him you made it here and he couldn't believe it," Morris said.

He helped me out of the cab and I followed him to a small back office. Old auto part books and yellow and white papers were piled up all over the desk. More books were on top of the file cabinets. Dirty mugs and a few overloaded ashtrays gave the office a nasty odor.

"This looks like a fire trap."

"Just be happy I'm lending you my cot, arsehole," Morris said.

Against the back wall was a green army cot with a grease-stained pillow. I collapsed onto it with a grunt and feel asleep.

CHAPTER TWENTY-TWO

I heard voices. Slowly I opened my eyes and found myself in the dirty auto shop office. Morris and Sean argued as I sat and moved my feet over the side of the cot.

I carefully touched my head and explored the tender spots where I had been smashed. When my fingertips found the lumpy cut just above my forehead, I gasped in pain.

"Hey, can you guys stop yelling and grab me some ice?" I asked, and picked at the dried blood on my cheek.

"No ice here, chief, but I'll get you some as soon as old Sean here stops giving me a bashing." Morris said, and turned to Sean, who was still outside the office.

"So, are you gonna get a fucking doctor or what?" I groaned.

"You don't need a doctor. Are you shot, Mister Conlin? Or is your skull broken?" Sean said, and stepped into the office, with his hunched over posture.

"I guess not, but since my cut stopped bleeding I'll be alright. Some ice sure would be neighborly."

"Well then, go get this boyo some ice, Morris," Sean ordered.

"Fine, I'll be right back. You need anything else?" Morris asked me.

"Yeah, I could really use some Bourbon," I said.

"Alright, let me see what I can find."

The door slammed behind him as he rushed out and the sound went right through my skull like a spike.

Sean leaned over me and brushed his white bangs out of his face.

"You fucked up my truck pretty damn good, lad. I guess it's okay since you got the gun shipment back here after all."

"Guns?" I asked.

"You mean Doyle didn't tell you? These are weapons, explosives and ammunition. It's too bad about that last shipment. We needed that, too. Our buyers are going be livid," he said, with a frown.

"They could've easily blown me to bits along with the shipment."

"Correct, Mister Conlin. Serious business with dangerous people. Those Gallagher fellows don't mess around. You're a lucky man to be alive."

"I know where the other shipment is."

"You do?"

"I'll need another truck and better weapons than a handgun with a few bullets." I said, reaching for my waistband, but came out with nothing. "Where's my gun?" I barked frantically.

"Relax lad, it was in the truck on the passenger seat. Here you go," he said, and handed me the pistol. "We'll need to call up Doyle before taking on the Gallaghers on their turf," Sean said, brushing the hair out of his eyes.

"So do it. We don't have much time to fuck around."

I got up and took a few steps only to stumble back down onto the cot. The whole room began to swim and I sat still waiting for the wooziness to pass.

After a while Morris came back with a brown bag.

He burst into the room like an excited child.

"Here ya go, mate. Look in the bag. Go ahead." He shoved the bag into my lap.

I peered in and found a bottle of Maker's Mark on top of a plastic bag of ice.

"This is awesome, Morris. You've done great. Thanks," I said, and placed the whole bag of ice over the top of my head.

Immediately the ice started melting in rivulets that ran down my face and all over my shirt. The numbing cold was a welcome relief from the dull ache in my head. I opened the bourbon and took a big swig. It warmed my chest and left a lasting burn on my tongue for a few seconds.

I held up the bottle to Morris who was still staring at me while I took another deep pull on the bottle. Unexpectedly he began to frantically search for something in his drawers and slammed a couple before he found his prize.

"Here it is!" he declared, and handed me an old fashioned glass.

"Thanks Morris. I appreciate it. You sure you don't

want a couple of fingers worth?"

"Alright, a quick nip before Sean comes back."

I poured two fingers of bourbon into the glass and handed it to him. He drank it down too fast, and coughed and choked a little before recovering. Maker's Mark wasn't one of the strongest bourbons, but it still had kick.

Just then, Sean showed up at the door. Morris quickly opened the desk drawer, dropped the glass in, and shut it just as fast.

"What's going on in here?" Sean asked. His eyes darted from me to Morris, and then he frowned.

"Oh nothing," Morris said.

Sean looked back and forth between us again.

"What's up?" I asked.

"There's something you need to see," said Sean.

"Let's have a look," Morris said, and quickly stood up.

We then both followed Sean to the back of the open truck.

"Climb up and have a look," Sean said.

He moved to the right and I climbed in. To my

shock and surprise the truck was completely empty.

"Doyle is gonna have an aneurism. Where are the crates?" Sean asked.

"I… I… don't know. Let me think a sec." Paralyzed with fear and horror, my mind swirled with confusion.

"Doyle's gonna skin you, boyo," Sean said.

I jumped down and rubbed my face.

"This can't be happening."

"Did you leave the truck unattended at any point?" Morris asked.

"You'd better leave town," Sean said.

"I can't, I just need better weapons than this handgun."

"Oh I see. They bashed you and took the crates. Didn't they?" Sean asked.

My eyes darted side to side as I tried to come up with an excuse, but it was no use. I sighed and told the truth.

"I'm sorry, they did knock me out, but I didn't know they took everything. I feel horrible. I'm sorry."

"Sorry ain't gonna cut it with Doyle," Sean said.

Morris walked to the other side of the garage and uncovered a crate.

"Take what you want from here," Morris said.

"What are you doing?" Sean asked, incredulous.

"I'm giving him a fighting chance," Morris shot back. Then he handed me a crowbar and stepped back.

I pried the crowbar under the edge and pulled back with all my weight. The crate made a loud crack as the nails pulled out of the wood. The lid splintered in spots as I pried around the edges until it popped open.

I slid the lid over the side and brushed away the wood chips. I then reached inside the crate and pulled out the first thing my hand felt. It was a cold metal tube. To my surprise I'd pulled out a handheld, rocket-propelled grenade launcher. The rockets lay right next to it, along with some rifles and ammunition.

I hadn't seen an RPG in years. "This will work. Thanks," I said, and smiled. It was hard to hold back my love of my old military life. At this point it almost seemed normal in comparison. I reached into my jacket for a cig and lit one up. The flame flared and I dragged deep on it, getting prepared for a war. It brought me back to my past in the military as a flash of images raced through my mind.

"Do you have another truck?" I asked.

"What do ya need another truck for?" Sean inquired.

"Well, you do want the shipment back? Right?" I countered.

"Oy, you're right. Morris will go with you," he said.

Sean smacked Morris on the back and he jumped.

"What? Me? No fucking way. I'm no gunslinger," Morris said. His face went completely white and I thought he was going to pass out, but he just sighed.

"Well someone has to help our friend recover and load up the truck. It's not going to be me, mate."

"Don't worry, Morris," I said. "You can drive and stay in the truck until I need you. But a gun might be a good idea just in case someone tries to mess with you."

"Go on, Morris. Stop being such a wanker. Be a man."

"Fuck off, Sean," Morris said, getting agitated.

"It'll be alright," I said.

"These are the fuckin' Gallaghers. How is this alright?" Morris asked. He coughed on his spit, his face turning bright red as he caught his breath.

We went through the crates and I gathered the weapons and ammunition. Sean handed Morris a small caliper pistol, a .22. He stood frozen with it in his opened hand.

"Just put it in your waistband," I told him. "Remember, it's just in case."

"Alright, Bill," he said.

"You have fired a gun before?" I asked.

"Yes, I just don't like them."

"You'll like having it if one of these creeps start shooting at you," Sean said.

"That's right," I said. "Oh, and Sean, one thing I forgot to tell you."

"Yeah?"

"You're coming too, mate."

I shoved an AK-47 and a clip into his chest.

"You're daft," he said.

"Listen, Sean, crazy's all we got. You and Morris

are my crew so start acting like it."

I opened a box of 7.76x39 rounds and loaded thirty into each clip. When I'd finished we had three magazines for each of us.

"Keep the safety on and don't forget to take it off," I said.

"This is crazy. I haven't shot a gun in twenty years," Sean said.

"Well, we wouldn't have to do this if you would've taken care of the Gallaghers before I got here," I reminded him.

"Where's that whiskey?" Sean asked.

Morris handed him the bottle. He took a big swig, let out a gasp, and wiped his mouth with the back of his shaky hand.

"This'll get me nerve up," he said.

All three of us piled into the cab of the truck and crammed in shoulder to shoulder. Morris started it up and we drove out of the garage bay. I pulled out my phone and routed the trip. When the phone started giving directions in a woman's voice, Morris jumped out to close the garage door and Sean flinched.

"What is that?"

"It's a smartphone."

"It talks?"

I nodded.

"I gotta get me one of those. If I live through this," Sean said.

Morris got back in the cab and let out a snicker. Sean elbowed him in the ribs and put the truck in gear.

"Hey watch it, that hurts," Morris complained.

"That'll teach ya."

Morris rubbed at his rib.

"Do you have one of those things?" Sean asked.

"No," Morris replied.

"Then shut your hole."

After that exchange, all was quiet for a while, each of us lost in our own thoughts.

We finally pulled up to the Gallaghers' warehouse, a large building with a black roof, big front windows, and loading docks in the front. The streets was deserted with abandoned warehouses and boarded up storefronts. There were a few cars and trucks in the parking lot but the three garage doors were closed. A black metal fence surrounded the property and the streets around the place were deserted.

"Crash the gate," I said.

"Brilliant," Morris cheered.

"What? You'll ruin my truck!" Sean barked.

"Don't think, just do it," I said.

The truck plowed through the gate and bucked with the impact. We were jolted forward and Sean grabbed onto my jacket.

"Everybody out!" I yelled.

"Stop shoving me," Sean grunted.

I pushed him out of the truck, then grabbed the equipment from behind the seats and handed Sean a rifle. I took out the RPG launcher and loaded the rocket with a turn and a click.

Just then, five men rushed out of the warehouse and fired pistols at the truck. Sean scurried for cover as bullets pinged off the side. I rested the RPG on the hood of the truck, aimed, and pulled the trigger. The launcher erupted with a shudder and a whoosh. The rocket sailed into the middle garage door, a white stream trailing behind it. It crashed into the garage with a ground-shaking explosion, a white hot flash of fire and black smoke. The men were blown off their feet and lay unconscious on the loading dock. The garage door was reduced to a smoldering hole.

"Let's finish this!" I yelled, and Morris and Sean looked on in shock, their mouths agape and eyes wide with fear.

"Hey, snap out of it. Back it up to the dock and let's get our stuff." They didn't move. "Morris! C'mon man. We don't have much time."

He blinked, turned to me, and then ran over to the truck.

Morris climbed into the truck and backed it up to the dock.

I jumped up onto the dock and kicked pieces of the shattered garage door out of my way. Inside were about ten wooden crates, which were similar to our missing ones. I searched the loading dock and found a crowbar. I cracked open one of the crates with a couple of grunts. Inside, wood shavings and that oily metal odor drifted up. I pushed the shavings aside and found weapons and ammo.

"I'm not sure all of this is ours, but let's take it. Morris, help me load these into the truck. We have to hurry."

Sean kept a nervous watch while we loaded the crates into the truck.

"Shout if you see anyone coming." I said.

"Alright, but hurry," Sean urged.

I glanced over at the men on the ground and couldn't tell if they were still alive, but no one stirred. We rushed to load all the crates. Sean came around, back bowed, with his rifle in hand.

"That's not all ours."

He struggled to lift his head and peeked at us as we finished up.

I peered at the writing on the crates. "Looks like Russian," I said.

We loaded the last of the crates in the truck, pulled down the truck's back door, and locked the latch.

"Hurry up. Get in. We gotta go!" I yelled.

I jumped into the driver's seat, gunned the engine, and threw the truck into first gear. Morris shoved Sean up into the cab with a grunt and climbed in behind him. I throttled the engine and it roared to life. We raced out into the street. I peered into the rearview mirror, paranoid that we might be followed, but the streets were deserted.

"The Gallaghers are gonna be pissed," I said. I shifted again and the truck jerked forward a little faster.

"They'll be more than a little pissed. They're gonna be irate," Sean said.

"We're not going back to the auto shop," Morris said. "Head back to Blackrock. We'll leave the truck with some of Doyle's boys. I'll tell you where to go."

After a while we arrived at The Missing Swan. It was a poorly lit, two-story brick building that was painted white. It had a row of small windows on the second floor and a tiny sign that was barely visible from the road.

We pulled around the back, into a pitch-black parking lot and I turned on the brights to cut the darkness as we parked. Morris and Sean climbed out and jumped down.

"We'll be right back," Sean said, slamming the truck

door shut.

They descended a set of basement stairs and disappeared.

I sat in the truck, exhausted, and drifted off into my own thoughts. I wanted to see Janette again. I wanted to kiss her full, pouty lips and feel her warm body against mine. I pictured her face and closed my eyes for a second. Then a loud bang on the passenger window startled me back to the present situation. Outside, three hulking men with black leather jackets and close-cropped hair stood glaring in at me. In the unlit lot it was hard to make out any features other than their size, but they looked menacing.

"Get out!" one barked and pulled on the locked door.

"Unlock it!" another demanded.

I was just reaching for my Berretta when Sean and Morris appeared with another guy.

"C'mon, Bill. Let these boys unload the truck," Sean said.

When the crates were unloaded, I started up the truck again. We dropped Morris off at his shop and I grabbed the bottle of bourbon. Then Sean and I headed back to his warehouse.

By the time we got back to the warehouse it was late and I was completely spent. I parked and we got out. Sean waddled towards the door, turned, and stuck out his hand. We shook and I walked over to the VW.

"I gotta tell you, mate. I was wrong. You don't look like much, but I'm impressed. You did a brilliant job today. I'll let Doyle know how things went. Expect a call from him."

I unlocked Tommy's red VW GTI, got in, and collapsed into the driver's seat. I rolled down the window, fired up a cig, and took a long drag as I searched the black sky for an answer to when this would end. I took a deep breath and slowly let out the smoke.

A flash of images from the day's events raced across my mind like a slide show. I pulled on the cig, and the tip glowed bright in the darkness. I finished the cig, closed my eyes, and thought about calling Janette, but I never got the chance. A soft rhythmic sound filled my ear from off in the distance and I fell into a deep slumber.

CHAPTER TWENTY-THREE

A cool breeze caressed my face from the slightly open window and I awoke to a bright morning. In the distance, heavy steel-colored clouds swallowed sunbeams, which dashed my hopes for sunshine and ushered in another dreary day.

I had cramped up with a pain between my shoulder blades, thanks to spending the entire night in the car. I lit up a cig and started up the GTI. I left the warehouse and turned onto Route 118, Merrion Road, heading north towards Janette's place.

Twenty minutes later I was in the heart of Dublin's Cork Hill with breakfast on my mind. My stomach gurgled and growled for coffee, eggs, and toast as I rolled into Janette's neighborhood and searched the streets for a place to park.

I called Janette's number. Her phone rang five times before it went to her voicemail. "This is Janette, you know what to do."

I left a message.

A few minutes later my phone buzzed with a few text messages from Janette: *Got an early class. I'll ring you around eleven. :-)*

I drove around on Dame Street and looked for a coffee place. After a while I pulled over and parked. I launched the Yelp app on my phone and searched for breakfast place. The Queen of Tarts had four and a half stars from over two hundred people so I headed over to check it out.

The cool, damp weather gave me a chill, so I zipped up my jacket and strolled down the street. The Queen of Tarts was a few blocks from where I'd parked and I did a bit of window-shopping along the way. Trendy shops and restaurants lined both sides of the street. I turned the corner by a cool comic and collectable store called Ink and spotted the breakfast place in the middle of the next block.

As I stepped inside, I was overtaken by the awesome morning activities. The aromas of coffee, pastry, and bacon made me drool. A long, clear glass showcase displayed desserts of all kinds. Cakes, tarts, and other pastries were piled high. There were so many standing trays and plates that not one inch of the display case were uncovered. I wanted to eat it all.

The place was packed with people sitting at small wooden tables.

An attractive redhead in her sixties greeted me. She rushed around taking orders with a tray in one hand and a red teapot in the other.

"Table for one please?"

"Sit wherever you can find a spot, darlin'. I'll be with you shortly," she said, and raced off.

I took a table on the first level and found a menu tucked between a creamer and sugar bowl. I decided to have something called the Hearty Breakfast, which looked like the biggest meal on the menu.

The waitress returned, placed a mug with a small pot of coffee on the table, and took out an order pad.

"I'm sorry, darlin', did you want coffee?"

"Yeah that's great. And I'll have the Hearty Breakfast."

"Coming right up," she said, and took off again.

I added cream to my coffee, sipped, and relaxed.

"Simple pleasures," I thought.

I spaced out, entranced by the activity and watched folks enjoying the food. Then my phone buzzed in my pocket. I pulled it out and read a text message from Janette.

Where R U?

Queen of Tarts.

Love that place. On way.

I took a few pictures with my phone and sent them to Janette.

Jealous?

Stop it, you dog, I'm almost there!

I didn't know her at all but I felt like there was something special about Janette. I was looking forward to seeing her again. While I waited for my food, I thought about meeting her at the pub and quickly drifted to the night of hot sex we shared. Was it her perfume or shampoo that made me so crazy? I couldn't decide, but all I knew was I felt a desperate need to get her alone again.

The waitress came over with my order and brought me back to the current moment. My plate was loaded with eggs, sunny side up, bacon, sausage, potato chive cake, and buttered toast. I put jam on my toast and started devouring the food.

I couldn't wait for Janette. I ate everything on my plate at a furious pace. At one point I looked up to see a couple of college girls staring at me. When our eyes locked they giggled and whispered. I gave them a quick smile, then put my head down and went back to work shoveling food into my mouth.

When I finished eating, I paid the bill and headed outside, unsure of what happened to Janette. I looked up and down the street, but didn't see her.

I fired up a cig and started walking back to the car. I reached into my pocket and pulled out my phone to text her. Just then, I noticed a stunning platinum blonde in a black leather jacket, blue jeans, and white converse high-top sneakers looking at me. Her hair was cut short and she wore bright red lipstick. I stared speechless, unable to look at my phone as it buzzed with messages from Janette.

The blonde walked past me and completely ignored my gaze. She then stopped to look into the window of the Queen of Tarts, then took out her phone and started texting. My phone buzzed with another message from Janette: *You're so thick.*

I lifted my head up to find the blonde was now standing in front of me, with a big grin.

"Wow! You look amazing." I was stupefied.

She looked absolutely gorgeous. Her transformation was spectacular. I grabbed her and pulled her in to a long kiss. Immediately that familiar perfume drove me crazy.

"You look good enough to eat," I said.

"C'mon, Bill, you're such an idiot."

"I don't know what to say other than, I feel lucky."

She smiled a little shyly, and then nuzzled my neck.

She took my hand, weaved our fingers together, and squeezed.

"Let's go to my place."

She yanked my arm and pulled me off balance down the street.

"My car is the other way," I said.

"Oh, now you have a car? How did that happen?"

"A gift from my employer."

"Really? Sounds a bit shady."

We walked around the block and stopped at the bright red VW GTI.

"He must like you a lot," she said.

"It's a long story, but it's actually his son's car. I'm only borrowing it for a while."

"Works for me," she said, with a smirk.

We got into the car and took off towards Janette's flat. I had just backed into a parking spot when my phone buzzed in my pocket. I struggled to get the call, but the phone got caught on the edge of my pocket and the buzzing stopped. I missed Mulligan's call.

I sighed nervously when the phone buzzed again and this time I answered it immediately.

"Who is that?" Janette asked.

"It's my boss," I replied.

I held my finger to my lips to quiet her and she frowned as I answered the call.

"Hello."

"Bill?"

"Yes, sir."

"I need to speak to you straightaway."

"I'm on my way. I'll be there within the hour."

"Good," he said, and ended the call.

I turned to Janette.

"I gotta go. I'll call you later. Maybe we can grab dinner?"

"Your loss," she said, then gave me a pouty look and hopped out of the car. She walked over to my side and kissed me through my open window. Her lips felt full, soft, and warm.

"Bye," she said, and walked off.

I pressed down the clutch, shifted into gear, and pulled away from the curb.

CHAPTER TWENTY-FOUR

When I arrived at Mulligan's farm, I parked in the driveway and stepped out of the GTI thinking of Janette, her perfume still lingering in my mind. I missed having a normal life and a home. I closed my eyes and took a deep breath as it started to rain. There was an aroma of peat and grass that will always remind me of Mulligan's base.

I walked up to the front door of the farmhouse and knocked. Doyle Mulligan opened the door with a big smile on his face. When I stepped inside, he grabbed me in a big bear hug. His cologne smothered me as much as his crushing grip. He released me, with his hands on my shoulders and stared straight into my eyes.

"You did it, boyo," he said.

"The shipment?" I asked.

"Let me tell you something, my young friend. That was very impressive work. I've never heard old Sean throw out so many compliments before. That old dodger loves you. I can't believe you made that crabby bastard carry a rifle and come along on the job. That's absolutely hilarious. Hilarious!" he bellowed.

Mulligan let out a deep, throaty laugh that turned into a coughing fit. His face turned red, until he regained control and cleared his throat.

"I'm just glad we were able to get your things back," I said.

"So humble. I like that. Well, I've got a surprise for you. C'mon, come see in the back." I followed him down the long hallway.

"Those crates had much more than just our stuff. That'll teach those hooligans. They're gonna be besides themselves for quite a while," Mulligan said.

He walked into his office, sat behind his large desk, and leaned back in his leather chair.

"Sorry, sir, I'm not sure I understand," I said.

Chief Gerry Alleyn sat in a chair on the right side of the office, twisting an unlit cigar in his mouth.

"There was a crate with twenty bricks of white powder. It's cocaine and all that shite is worth a lot of money. What an incredible find, absolutely brilliant. I made sure none of my men came to investigate the explosion, at least for a bit. Can't stop the local busy bodies for long," Chief Gerry said.

Doyle Mulligan slapped his desk with both hand and roared with laugher. I flinched from the outburst. Chief Gerry and Mulligan continued to laugh. It was so contagious that I couldn't help but joined in.

"I guess those brothers are gonna be a little upset," Mulligan boasted.

"Upset? That's an understatement," Chief Gerry blurted.

Mulligan waved his hand in the air and dismissed the notion with a smile. His energy was infectious and I smiled so much my jaw ached. I hadn't ever seen him this elated. Mulligan turned around and opened a file cabinet behind him. He took out a fat white envelope and pushed it across the desk.

"Here you go, lad. Well earned."

I picked up the white envelope, lifted the flap, and peeked inside. My eyes locked, transfixed by several stacks of purple-pink five hundred euro notes. I thumbed through the notes and realized that I now had what I needed to move on. I could leave, contact Yuri, and gather a crew to take on Viktor. The only problem was Janette. She was addictive. As much as I wanted to kill Viktor I struggled with the notion of losing her.

"Thank you, sir. This is very generous."

"You'd better put that in a safe place, son. Oh, and that's not all. Get whatever equipment you need to take care of your situation with the Russians."

His eyes shifted from my shocked expression to Chief Gerry.

"I don't know what to say. Thank you."

He came around the desk and sat on the edge. He smacked me on the back. "I'm the one who owes you a debt of gratitude. Listen, there's a big fight coming up at the gym. It's Tommy's next-ranked fight and there's a bunch of other great fighters on the card too. Please come as my guest."

He walked back to the cabinet, pulled open a drawer, and handed me two bright green tickets spotted with a clovers.

"Next Friday, at nine. And bring a date."

"We sir, I'm not sure I'll be here. I did want to deal with that Russian situation as soon as possible."

"Nonsense. What's the hurry? You have to stop and smell the flowers once and a while, boyo. If you need anything else call. Now get the fuck out."

He sat down behind his desk, smiled at Chief Gerry, and waited for me to leave.

"Thanks again, Mr. Mulligan."

"Hold onto Tommy's car until you leave town. I'll see you at the fight. Oh, and Bill, stay sharp out there. The Gallaghers are gonna be fuming for a quite a while."

I left his office, walked outside into the cool damp air, and closed the door behind me. I got into the GTI, started the engine, and glanced into the envelope as I tried to get a handle on the moment. A dark blur cut across my vision from the right. It was a swallow that darted in sharp turns like a fighter jet. It changed direction effortlessly and snatched its insect prey with a quick midair flit. I needed to stay flexible and think about changing my plans. Maybe I should hold off with my trip east until I see what developed with

Janette. I didn't want to lose her.

I got back on the road and headed north towards Janette's apartment. I passed a few small towns, but when my stomach growled I looked for a place to grab something to eat. When I passed a sign for a Domino's Pizza I pulled off. I ordered a pie and attacked it as soon as it came out, burning my palette after stuffing my face like an animal.

When I got back on the motorway, I realized the gas tank was near empty. I took the ramp off the M11 at Glenagerary and followed the signs to a Texaco station. After I filled up the tank, a black Benz pulled into the station close behind me. I glanced into the rearview mirror and noticed two rough-looking men in the front seat. Both stared back, stone faced, and didn't leave the sedan to gas up. They had shaved heads and wore two-tone nylon tracksuits with Nike emblems on the chest. Neither man moved or stepped out for anything, only stared straight like stone statues.

As I pulled away from the gas station, I saw them following me from my rearview mirror. I drove back onto the M11 and tried not to panic as I entered

Blackrock. The Benz stayed far behind, but didn't try to hide the fact that they were tailing me. I took the exit at Ashford and they followed after me. I gunned the accelerator and downshifted. The engine growled to life as the turbo kicked in and raced around a tight curve. I gave the engine more gas to gain some wiggle room.

"Let's see what this is about," I said.

I headed west for twenty minutes and got off on Route 755. At one point I thought I had lost them, but then they reappeared in my mirror.

I entered Laragh and raced through the town, as hills and trees blurred past like a green paint smear. I entered Glendadough and noticed a visitor center coming up, and then took a left onto Route 756 headed and deeper into a park. I passed a small lake on my left and a lodge, but the road brought me to a dead-end at a big lake with a large parking area.

I threw the white envelope into the glove box, locked it, and got out of the car. I wasn't going to need the money if I was dead, but didn't want it on me. With no Benz was in sight, I quickly dashed into the woods and ducked behind a tree. Carefully I stepped over scattered roots and crunched on dead leaves. I weaved through the underbrush and trees just outside the edge of parking lot and looked for cover. As I crept deeper into the woods, branches and leaves snapped and crackled under my feet, making it impossible to hide my location. I pulled out the Beretta 9mm from my waistband, took a deep breath, and leaned my back against a thick tree.

I peeked around the trunk to survey the lot, but there was no sign of trouble. I panted, as beads of sweat gathered on my forehead and dripped in rivulets down the side of my face. My heart throbbed in my throat, and I braced myself for whatever was coming.

After a while I calmed down. There still was no sign of the thugs in the parking area. The only noises were birds and the wind as it blew through the treetops. I heard leaves rustle behind me and spun around low with my gun out front. I slid to the ground in a prone position and listened, intent on identifying the direction of the next noise. I lay completely motionless with my Beretta 9mm out at arms' length and aimed down the sites with my breath held.

I scanned the tree line about fifty feet away. A twig snapped loudly, followed by tense silence. My entire body broke into a hot sweat and I blinked furiously as sweat rolled into my eyes. It burned and blurred my vision for a few seconds, but I blinked it away and frantically wiped at my wet brow desperate to focus on the sound.

A small red squirrel with a white belly jumped up and hopped to a tree several feet to the left. It stopped, flicked its tail a few times, and bounced up a tree.

"Just a fucking squirrel?" I let out an uneasy breath and an awkward laugh.

I wiped at my eyes with the back of my wrist and waited, feeling like I wasn't alone. Seconds ticked by like minutes, the only thing I was able to focus on was my breathing.

Another sound came from my right and I turned sharply trying to identify the source. More rustling followed, but I couldn't figure out which direction it came from - it seemed to be coming from both sides. I felt tense and skittish not sure if it was my nerves or something more sinister.

Come on Bill, keep it together. I shook my head.

Without warning the ground around me erupted. Leaves and dirt exploded into the air. I rolled and scooted back behind a tree and panted heavily. A series of shots shattered the quiet forest. The gunfire echoed through the trees, as if someone had set off a pack of firecrackers. The tree trunk I leaned against exploded into splinters inches from my face. Wood shards flew into the air and stung my cheek. I frantically crawled away from my position as bullets whizzed over my head and hunkered down in a slight ditch behind another tree.

I peered around the bottom of the trunk and caught a glimpse of something white about thirty yards to my right. I took a deep breath, waited, and exhaled slowly with my hands steady. I aimed and focused on the edge of the tree hoping to see the white peek out again and when it did I pulled the trigger rapidly. A crimson mist sprayed into the air followed by a grunt and a final exhale.

From the corner of my eye I saw a large maroon

blur barreling towards me. He slammed into me hard and knocked me off my knees. I landed hard with a gasp. I struggled to catch my breath, but couldn't. It felt as if I was hit by a car. Seconds passed in slow motion as I gasped the sweet air into my lungs, which burned with the effort.

The stocky man jumped up fast and came at me again cursing in Russian as he lunged wildly. I spun around and sidestepped him and he blew past me like a passing train.

We stared at each other with eyes locked waiting to see who would make the first move. I glanced down and noticed he had black metal rod in his hand and just then he used it to make a wide chopping swing. I felt a white hot flash of pain as it grazed my temple, but I forced myself to stay on my feet as I staggered back a few feet from the blow. His arm came down fast again. The metal baton cut through the air with a whoosh and I intercepted his upper arm and threw him over my hip. He flipped into a tree trunk, bounced off, and scrambled to his feet ready for more.

The sky opened up and sheets of rain soaked the

dead leaves. The Russian charged at me again, but he tripped over a large root. He went down hard and his head thumped into a rock with a sickening wet smack. His forehead split open and dark red blood poured from his cracked skull. He lay completely still. I stood there for a few minutes in shock and panting, confused by this bizarre stroke of luck.

Then I walked over and felt his neck for a pulse, but found none. I searched his jacket for identification. All I found was an open soft pack of Lucky Strike cigarettes and a book of matches from a nightclub called Pravda. *Yuri's brand. I could have used his help, but I wasn't sure how that would go over with Mulligan. Ukrainians or Russians - he probably wouldn't trust him,* I thought to myself and nodded.

I put the cigarettes and matches into my pocket, and then made my way over to the other guy. He lay spread-eagle on his back, a golf-ball sized chunk missing from above his ear. His head looked like raw chopped meat.

Bile rose up and burned the back of my throat, but I swallowed it down hard. I knelt beside him and searched his body for clues. Inside his jacket pocket I found another pack of cigarettes and a red plastic lighter.

Unexpectedly both his hands shot up and squeezed my throat in a vise grip. I gasped for air as he crushed my windpipe. I grabbed at his hands, but couldn't budge them. His whole face grimaced with gritted teeth as he squeezed and grunted, giving it everything he had. I started to blackout. I scratched at his face in a fumbling attempt to stop him, but it was no use.

Desperate to release his hold on my throat, I grabbed at his skull and felt something wet and mushy. I jabbed my fingers deep into the hole in his head. He shook with a violent spasm that ravaged his body. Then his arms jutted out and reached for the heavens in a grotesque final gesture of death.

I collapsed onto the ground and vomited from the revolting struggle. I gulped air back into my burning lungs and tried to remain conscious as I searched the dead assassin's body.

I found a Russian driver's license and a Platinum American Express card. Roman Minin. I wiped my bloody hands on his white tracksuit and headed back to the parking lot.

CHAPTER TWENTY-FIVE

I reached the outskirts of Dublin as the sun left the sky with an orange and purple glow. When I reached for my phone to call Janette, I noticed dried blood on my hands and fingernails, which made me remember that the Russians knew this car and were tracking me. I couldn't put her in danger. The first thing I needed to do was to get rid of the GTI, so I called Sean.

"These fuckers tried to kill me," I barked.

"Slow down, lad. Who?"

"The Russians or the Gallaghers. They're tracking me. You gotta help me. Do something!" I screamed into the phone.

"Alright mate, take it easy. Let's get that car off the road. Bring it to Morris and I'll call Doyle and let him know your situation." Sean ended the call and I stared at the phone in disbelief. I let out a frustrated wail and sped over to the Crack Motor Shop.

When I arrived Morris already had the garage door open. I pulled straight in and he closed it immediately.

"Are you okay? Holy mother... What's with all that blood from? Why is your neck all marked up?" Morris asked, eyes wide in terror.

"Some Russian contract killers followed me into the woods. They tried to murder me, but I took care of them. I gotta get this blood off me quick. C'mon let's go."

"Let me shut down the shop and we'll go. I'll take the Volkswagen somewhere and deal with the bug tomorrow. We can head over to my flat and get you cleaned up. Take this whiskey. I'll meet you out front."

Morris handed me a small pint of Jameson then rushed around the room. He shuffled papers, as he frantically looked for something, and then he jingled a set of keys.

"Alright. Go outside and I'll be right there."

I stepped out front and reached for a cig. I came out with the dead man's Lucky Strikes and the Pravda matches.

"Better you than me," I said, aloud.

I took a deep swig from the bottle, then shook out a cig and lit up. The blue flame flared and went out leaving only a red glow in the darkness. I blew the smoke out and took another big gulp of the whisky. It burned as it went down and a boozy feeling dulled my anxiety. The whiskey was doing its job well and I puffed hard on my cig.

Morris pulled up in an old white Ford with a loud motor that sounded like a lawn mower. It was a nineteen-' Ford Escort in pristine condition. It looked like a car I'd seen in an old movie like *The French Connection* or *Dirty Harry*. Round headlights, chrome grill, and chrome push button door handles. I followed Morris and parked the GTI on the street a few miles from the shop and locked it up.

I stepped over to Morris' car, which actually had old-timey chrome roll-up window handles.

"She's forty-plus and still runs like a dream," Morris said, with pride.

"More like a nightmare," I countered and got in.

"My dad gave it to me when I was a lad. She's a great car."

"She sure is a miracle," I yelled, over the engine.

"What?" he shouted.

"I said that's awesome."

"Yes it is," he said.

Morris gunned the engine and we took off. As the motor sputtered down the road, every part of my body vibrated. I thought I was going to lose my mind from the loud engine and vibrating chassis until Morris pulled into a driveway of an old two-story light blue house. He drove back to the back and parked in front of a garage.

I climbed out of the car and could still feel a distant rumble in my feet from the vibrating engine. Morris led the way up a couple of stairs to a back porch with a windowed door that was peeling from having been painted too many times. He unlocked the door and we stepped into a kitchen that was a mess like Morris' office, with piles of dirty dishes in the sink and plates of half-eaten food scattered along the counters and on the round kitchen table.

"Sorry about the mess, but I don't get much company."

"That's okay, I used to live alone."

"The shower's upstairs. Follow me."

Morris ducked into a room and rifled through closets and drawers. After a while he reappeared with a stack of clothes and a dark brown towel.

I took a scalding hot shower in an old standing tub covered in black grease, but I didn't care. It felt phenomenal. I watched the blood and dirt spiral down the drain as hot water sprayed against my back and neck.

The stress left my body as the hot water washed over me, though I couldn't shake the horrible images of the dead assassins lying in the woods. The final image burned into the back of me eyelids – the assassin's arms straight out reaching towards the sky.

A few minutes later I dried off and put on Morris' clothes, a navy jumpsuit that he used for work with oil stains that wouldn't wash out. I left the towel on the edge of the tub and went downstairs to find Morris in his living room watching the news.

"Anything about Glendadough Lake?" I asked.

"Not a thing."

He gestured to the empty spot next to him. I sat down and the plastic-covered floral couch creaked in protest.

"Want something to drink?" He asked.

"What do you have?"

"Well, I don't have any Bourbon, but I've got some Jameson."

"That'll be fine." I said.

Morris went into the kitchen and returned with half a bottle of Jameson 12 year and two glasses. He poured three fingers into each glass and handed me one. Then he clinked the bottom of his glass into the top of mine.

"Sláinte. It's Irish and simply means, to good health."

"A girl I just met told me how to say it, but I suck."

"Try it."

"Sl-at-jah," I said.

He took another sip and smiled.

"Close, but not quiet right, mate. By the time we finish this bottle, you'll have it down."

The next morning we had a simple breakfast in Morris's dirty kitchen. He fried eggs with rashers and brewed up a large pot of tea. The food was a little greasy, but good. We finished up and Morris put the fry pan and dirty dishes in the sink.

"You want me to help clean up?" I offered.

"Nah, mate. You're my guest. I'll take care of this later."

We went back to the shop and waited for hours, but no word from Sean or Doyle. I helped out while he worked on cars by handing him tools. He told me the story of his life and how Doyle Mulligan saved the family's business when his dad was in trouble with the banks. They had generations of mechanics in the family and a love of cars that went back to the birth of automobiles. Grease was in their blood; they practically came out of the womb with black goop under their fingernails.

I was amazed when Morris showed me how he could identify problems with cars just by listening. I started up an old BMW. The car had an odd idle with a whine and within seconds of listening to the engine he knew exactly what to do. In less than an hour the engine was running smooth again.

Morris offered me his Ford to drive into town, but

there was no way I could jeopardize the love of his life. My history with keeping cars intact was very spotty lately and I couldn't take the chance of ruining the family heirloom.

Eventually Morris lent me a navy 1980s Audi 5000, which had just been fixed. It purred to life when I started the engine. He definitely had a knack for keeping crusty cars on the road.

I sent Janette a text that I was heading over. She responded that her day was full with an early Art History class, but had a break before an all-day painting session. I asked her to let me know when she'd finished and we'd grab some food.

I arrived at the center of Dublin and parked on the street in front of Janette's flat. I sat in the car and lit up a Lucky Strike with the matches from Pravda. I noticed some writing behind the cardboard matches: Wicklow to Blackrock twelve thousand euros, red VW GTI.

"What the fuck?"

The Gallagher's brought in talent from out of town to deal with me, but how did they know?

I rubbed the back of my neck and tried to think it through. Something felt wrong.

There had to be someone on the inside feeding them information. Who could it be? Maybe they followed or tracked me, but I never saw anyone. Paranoia and confusion swirled in my head.

"Oh shit! Morris." I blurted, started up the Audi and peeled out into traffic.

I raced over to the auto shop and found the door ripped open. There was a gaping, splintered hole where the lock had been and the entire place was in shambles. It had been ransacked and it made my stomach churn. An odor of excrement and urine assaulted my senses and I involuntarily gaged. Immediately I covered my nose and mouth with my hand and tried not to breathe through my nose, but the stench was overwhelming.

I took a quick glance around the shop. The cars in the bays had been decimated with smashed lights and windows. Pieces of red plastic and clear glass crunched under my feet as I stepped through the garage. Tools were thrown all over and some protruded out of the broken windscreens where they'd landed. Cans of oil were poured all over the floor and made for a slippery mess. I pulled out my Beretta 9mm and stepped carefully into Morris's office. I didn't think anyone was still here, but wasn't going to take any chances.

His office was empty and at first it looked like the same old mess as before, but it wasn't. The file cabinets were busted opened and most of the invoices and records were thrown all over the room.

I went around the back and found Morris' prized Ford Escort untouched, but there was no sign of Morris.

I went out front, sat against the wall and lit up a smoke. I squeezed the soft pack in my hand and threw them a few feet away.

"I fucking hate these crappy cigarettes," I said, aloud.

I pulled out my own hard pack of reds and lit up.

Thirty minutes later, a red tow truck with a loud engine pulled up. Morris flung open the door, shut off the engine and jumped down.

"How long you been waiting mate?"

"Where were you?" I asked.

"What's with the long face?

He surveyed the cigarette butts scattered on the ground around me.

"What's going on?"

"You're not gonna like it," I said. "Go on and take a look."

Then I took a deep drag of my cig and watched him rush into the shop.

"What happened to my door? Who did this? What's that fucking smell? Aww c'mon, this is putrid."

I heard a series of loud crashes and screams of frustration. He grunted in disgust and came out pissed off and panted as he tried to get some fresh air in his lungs. I glared at him and took another drag of my cig, and then flicked it away. He stared at me, his eyes wide.

"Where were you?" I asked again.

"I had to pick up parts and get rid of the GTI."

"It's a good thing no one was here otherwise you'd be dead," I said.

Tears of rage welled up in his eyes and he didn't say another word, just climbed into the truck, started the engine, and stared straight ahead. After a few minutes he gunned the accelerator a couple of times, and took off without a glance as he pulled out of the lot. The engine roared like an angry beast and the large black tires, kicked up gravel and dirt as he drove away. It hopped off the curb and left a gray cloud of exhaust in its wake.

CHAPTER TWENTY-SIX

Over the next several days, an eerie quiet replaced the dangerous exchange with the Gallaghers. I couldn't help but feel the anxious to leave when I thought about what Viktor had done to me. I'd have to find Yuri through his sister at her bed and breakfast in the Ukraine. Once there he could help me get over the border to Russia. Mulligan said he would help with weapons and transportation out of Ireland.

It felt like Janette and I were playing house, but I knew I had to leave her soon and this put a gloomy shadow over our lovers' bliss. I stayed at Janette's place and we became so close it felt like a normal life. Living together was like a sweet reprieve to my dangerous and depressing life. Small special moments of intimacy and tenderness formed a friendship I'd never had with a woman before. I looked forward to simple routines like morning coffee, waking together, and window-shopping. I became comfortable with her schedule and it was simply bliss.

At night I relaxed with Knob Creek, while Janette sketched out ideas for her independent painting class. She used thin pieces of charcoal that looked like black twigs and sketched on a small white pad, scribbles that days later became colorful wall-sized abstract paintings. The process was an intoxicating transformation of trial and error until she felt that she'd taken the designs far enough to stop. I drank it all in, like the bourbon I used to drown my past.

"Real soon I'll have gallery shows of my work. I'll make a killing."

She sat with a sketchpad on her crossed legs and her eyes drifted off daydreaming to that future moment of glory, and then smiled.

One night we went out to see her teacher's paintings at a local gallery. It was a year's worth of work and was supposed to be a big deal. Well, it was to Janette. She wanted me to understand her dream of what was possible and see what the art world was all about so I agree to go along.

We stepped out of her building and into the damp

night. A light misty rain hung in the air. After we had walked several of blocks, I noticed a black van with dark tinted windows shadowing us from a distance and I became extremely edgy.

"How far is this place?" I asked, as I glanced back.

"I don't know, another six blocks or so. Why? What's wrong?"

"Don't turn around, but I think we're being followed by that black van."

I pulled out the Beretta 9mm from my waistband and held it at my side.

"Are you serious? You seem so jumpy. Is that a bloody gun?" she asked, her eyes wide with shock.

The van caught up and the side door slid open. I frantically shoved Janette down behind a parked car and covered her with my body.

"Stop it. What is wrong with you?"

"Don't move," I barked.

The van slowly crept past, closed its side door, and turned right around the corner.

Janette squirmed out from under me and punched my hard in the chest.

"Don't ever do that again. Why are you being so weird tonight?"

"I'm sorry, I just thought someone was gonna... I mean..."

I didn't want to tell her what was really going on. I rubbed my chest where she'd punched me and searched the street for the van.

"Listen, if you don't want to go, just leave. You're not going to ruin this for me," she said, and marched off down the block.

"Wait, I'm coming!" I yelled.

I quickened my pace to catch up and grabbed her arm.

"Listen, there are some things you should know. I've had problems with some shady people. I think they're coming for me now."

"Do you have any idea how crazy you sound? What sort of problems?"

"I stole something and now they want it back. Actually, they stole it first from us first, well some of it, and now they want me dead."

"Really? That doesn't make any sense. Is that the

best you can come up with? What, so you're like an assassin?" she asked, jokingly.

"Yes."

She held up her hand with a scowl.

"Stop. You're such an asshole. I'm not dealing with this now. You'll have to play your games later. Put that gun away and let's go."

Janette headed into the gallery, which was packed with people. The gallery had high ceiling and large walls that showcased the enormous colorful paintings. Her teacher, Jason Collier, had created mural-size abstract paintings that filled the walls with striped worm-like creatures that crawled through smoky atmospheric clouds.

"I'm getting a drink," Janette said, and she stormed off.

For the rest of the event, Janette was cold as ice and wouldn't speak to me. At one point, I walked to the front of the gallery and stared out the ceiling-high windows, but the street was dead quiet. I watched Janette as she sipped wine, laughed, and chatted with people. I felt uncomfortable and self-conscious so I decided to step outside for a smoke.

Out on the stoop I chain-smoked and scanned the area for the black van, but it was gone. Occasionally I'd glanced inside to see what Janette was up to, but couldn't get her to look my way. Cigarette butts lay scattered on the ground around me like dead soldiers. I looked into my hard pack and realized I only had one cig. I ambled south a few streets and found a small store that sold cigarettes and magazines.

I bought two packs of Marlboro Reds and stepped out into the street. I smacked the hard pack's bottom a couple of times, pulled off the plastic wrapper, and the silver foil lip inside. I licked my lips and screwed a cig into my mouth, then noticed another black van. It rolled slowly down the street and I watched intently as it drove by.

Its side door slid open and a man dressed in black with a baklava turned towards me and opened fire. Flashes of fire came from his sub machine gun as it spit bullets that peppered the block. Dozens of bullets pinged and ripped through the cars in front of me. After a few seconds a massive explosion erupted with a stunning fireball that rained sparks and glass all around me. I ducked down low and ran back towards the gallery. The assassin sprayed the cars again in a desperate effort to take me out, but I dove onto the sidewalk and his shots whizzed over my head.

Everything stopped with a sudden series of clicks when the assassin paused to reload. I peeked up over a car's roof and fired my Beretta 9mm rapidly into the van's opening. My first volley sparked off the side door, but one bullet managed to hit the assassin in the shoulder and knocked him back.

The driver accelerated and sped off, the rear wheels smoked and screeched against the wet pavement. I aimed at the driver's window and unloaded my entire clip until a bright red splash of blood hit the front windscreen. The van went out control and careened off some parked cars and then slammed hard into a light post and came to a dead stop, with flames and smoke bellowing from the damaged engine. A few seconds later it exploded in a bright flash of heat that lit up the night sky and reflected off the stores and cars. The impact shattered store windows, including those of the gallery, and glass shards sprinkled the street.

I ejected the empty magazine. It clattered onto the ground and I snapped another one home and chambered a round.

The gallery emptied out into the street with shouts and panicked cries of concern and horror. Janette stared at the flaming wreck and her eyes snapped to me. I ran across the street, grabbed her wrist and we ran towards my parked Audi. She stumbled along without a word, eyes locked on the smoldering hull. The fire department arrived with lights and sirens blaring and immediately sprayed water on the flaming wreck.

A second black van barreled down the road towards the calamity. Janette and I finally reached the car and jumped in without looking around. I quickly drove away from the curb and glanced in the rearview mirror. The van quickly raced in reverse. I shifted wildly through the gears and turned sharply down a side street, the tires whined in protest. I managed to shake them for a moment and hurriedly dropped

Janette off at her flat.

"I have to ditch this car far away from here. I'll be back in a while."

"Just hurry!" she said, and slammed the car door hard, a sour expression on her face. I waited for her to go into her building and kept watch in my rearview mirror. Once she was safe inside I peeled out to hide the car.

The spot I picked was a couple of miles north, by the River Liffey. I found a large office building and pulled around back. I sat in the dark and tried to get a handle on what had just happened. Two black vans with assassins and they knew where to find me again How? I needed to find out what the hell was going on.

I left the Audi and quickly started back to Janette's place. It was late and the streets were dark and empty. The cold misty air kept me sharp, alert, and jumpy.

Thirty minutes into my walk the sky opened up and rain soaked me to the bone. Black puddles like giant oil slicks saturated my path back and the dark pavement soon became flooded inches deep.

When I reached Janette's street I approached it

carefully anticipating another ambush, but the streets were deserted. I still took my time and inspected her block warily, but with no signs of trouble I ducked into her building a nervous wreck and completely exhausted as she buzzed me in.

I was thoroughly soaked to the bone. My boots squeaked loudly on the tiled floor and water seeped out of the lace holes with each step I took. A chill shook me violently as I stepped inside Janette's flat.

CHAPTER TWENTY-SEVEN

Janette was totally pissed off. I hadn't seen this side of her before, but I sort of liked it. Her intense expressions and fiery eyes were a turn on.

"Please, I just want to take a hot shower and then I'll answer all your questions." I headed into the bathroom, turned on the water in the shower, and looked in the mirror.

"What was that? Tell me now," she demanded, following me into the bathroom.

"I told you what was happening, but you didn't believe me."

"I was gonna tell you to get lost, when you started acting all nuts and pushed me down, but after the gun shots and the explosion... Now I don't know what to say."

"Give me a few minutes and we'll talk. I promise."

Janette collapsed on the toilet. She sat with her arms folded and stared at nothing, a blank expression on her face.

"I don't understand. I mean… you said they were coming, but how did you know?"

I took off my wet smoky smelling clothes. "I knew it was just a matter of time. I've dealt with ruthless people before and they don't give up."

I got in the shower and shampooed my hair then rinsed out the suds. I picked up the soap and lathered my body.

"Will they? Umm… try to kill me too?"

"Anything is possible, but not if I can help it."

"I want a gun. Teach me. Teach me how to shoot."

"No way. Are you serious?"

"Are you sure I can't convince you," Janette said.

She pulled the shower curtain aside. She stepped in and rubbed her beautiful curves against my soapy body.

That night I slept hard, exhausted from the day's events. I awoke to a scratching sound, opened my eyes and listened intently, but the scratching abruptly stopped. I lay in bed and tried to identify the direction of the sound. Then it started again this time at a frantic pace. I jumped out of the bed and searched the apartment for its source. I went into the living room, and thought I was getting closer, but then it stopped again. A black cat with a brown leather collar sat outside on the window ledge. It scratched at the frame, flicking its tail.

I walked into the kitchen, opened the refrigerator, and poured milk into a bowl. The milk came out too fast and spilled all over the counter. I went back to the window, but the cat was gone and the milk in the bowl had unexpectedly turned black. The scratching started again this time in the bedroom. I took the bowl and headed to find the cat. The milk sloshed and spilled as I walked, leaving a black trail behind me.

The bedroom window was open, but I didn't remember leaving it that way. Rain blew into the room, pooling on the floor, so I closed it. The cat was in the bed next to Janette, but I couldn't believe my eyes and shook my head in horror. The cat laid dead, its neck twisted at an unnatural angle with grotesquely large eyes. Its fangs were bared and its tongue hung loose to the side.

I looked on in shock as the cat twitched and rotated its head in my direction. It began to cry out in agony, with a sinister shrill so loud that pain shot through my ears. I dropped the bowl of black milk and it smashed into shards that cut into my feet. The cat continued to shriek and I covered my ear from the piercing cries, but the pain was too much and forced me to my knees. I knelt in a puddle of what I thought was split milk, but it was now dark red blood. The dark puddle rippled and began to swirl into a vortex.

Some unknown force grabbed my ankles in a vise grip and yanked me down. The vortex swirled over around me. I was waist-deep in the dark liquid and I struggled as it pulled me down deeper. I clawed and scratched at the edges of the floor, but it was no use. The blood had reached my neck and filled my mouth. I thrashed to keep my head above the surface, but started to drown. I tried to catch one last big breath as my face descended below the surface for the last time. My mind filled with panic as I suffocated unable to breathe. I let out one last shriek for my life.

"No!" I screamed with every bit of my being and

shot out of bed in a cold sweat. I shivered with my back against the wall, t-shirt soaked through and my head still feeling suffocated by the blood.

"What's wrong? It's just a dream. Come here," Janette said.

She tried to calm me, but I wouldn't go anywhere near the bed.

"I couldn't breathe," I said.

Frantically I searched the bedroom for the black cat, the broken bowl, or the blood from my dream, but it was only in my head. I took a deep breath and let it out in a frightened shutter and tried to calm myself down. I put on a dry t-shirt, walked out into the living room and stayed on the couch until morning.

Sunlight beamed into my eyes and I awoke to the familiar smell of strong coffee, eggs, and toast. Janette had covered me during the night with a red blanket and I pulled it over my head to partially block the sunlight that radiated through the windows. The images from my nightmare were still fresh in my head. I couldn't feel the tugging anymore, but I could still see the cat's hideous face.

"Sorry, we're out of rashers."

She placed the breakfast on the table in front of the couch.

"Want me to fix your coffee?" she asked.

"Nah, I'll get some," I said.

I sat up and rubbed at my eyes. I felt slow and foggy, as if I hadn't slept at all, but tried to shake it off.

"Are you alright? I've never heard anyone scream out like that."

"Yeah, that was bad. I couldn't stop it."

"Stop what?"

"The blood in the nightmare."

"Someone was bleeding? Was it you or...?" Her voice trailed off.

"I was drowning. It was so horrible."

I closed my eyes and shook my head in disbelief. I went into the kitchen, grabbed a mug, and poured some coffee. The aroma of the coffee helped me wake up. I opened the refrigerator and took out the cream, and had a flash behind my eyes of the cat with its twisted head and bulging eyes. I dropped the container of cream and it exploded on the floor. I cleaned up the mess then poured cream into my mug as the nightmare image faded. I watched the cream swirl in the coffee in my mug.

"Where's your gun?" Janette asked.

"Why?"

"I want to hold it."

I made sure the safety was on, pointed it down, and handed it to her.

"Wow, it's heavy. What's that button you just hit?"

She weighed it in her hand and flipped it over.

"It's the safety. You need to switch it off to shoot."

"Dark, shiny, and powerful. I'm going to add it into my paintings." She handed it back with a smirk.

"We can go into the woods and shoot it sometime soon. Aiming takes some getting use to."

My phone buzzed loudly and I saw it was Mr. Mulligan. I placed the gun on the counter and quickly answered.

"What's up, sir?" I asked.

"We need to chat, lad. There have been some new developments. Come over now."

"I've had some serious developments too," I said, but he had already ended the call.

CHAPTER TWENTY-EIGHT

An hour later the taxi pulled up at Mulligan's farm. Light snow flurries fell from a lead-colored sky. The snow had started to stick and coated the road. About ten cars and SUVs were parked on the grass and along the cobblestone wall.

I climbed out of the taxi, paid the driver, and zipped up my jacket. The cold wind bit at my cheeks and the snowflakes felt like frozen needles when they landed on my skin. Cars blocked Mulligan's driveway and the iron gate was closed. Two monstrous sentries glared at me from behind the gate. They were taller and wider than me, with long black leather jackets and sub machine guns peeking out from their open coats.

I walked up to the gate and they growled like feral dogs with teeth bared.

"What are you about?" The left sentry pointed the barrel of his gun in my direction.

"Mulligan wants to see me. I'm Bill," I said.

An awkward silence filled the dead air while they stared at me for what felt like minutes, but no one moved.

One took out a phone from his jacket and pressed a button.

"Some wee American bloke wants to see Mulligan. Yeah, says his name is Bill. Right."

He put the phone away and opened the gate.

I stepped inside and walked past them without looking back. A nervous trigger finger could accidentally spray a whole clip into me in a fraction of a second.

The front door handle was unlocked and the inside of the house was booming with voices. It sounded like a party, with countless men laughing and speaking at the same time. The living room was packed. When I entered the main room, all went silent and eyes burned on me. I immediately became self-conscious and nodded my head as a greeting to the unwelcome attention. Their heads turned back just as quickly resuming their conversations and the room once again filled with noise. Clearly no one saw me as a threat, but I could've mowed down the big idiots with one machine gun clip.

I weaved my way to the hallway that led to Mulligan's office. Sean hurried over and pulled me aside.

"C'mon Doyle needs you."

He struggled to lift his head and made eye contact with me for a brief second, and then led the way to Mulligan's office.

Tommy came out of the waiting area out the office with a sour expression.

"What the bloody hell is that fuckin' bastard doing here? I can go find those fuckers," he hissed.

"Take it easy Tommy. Your Da needs to do the sorting on this. Don't make things worse. Settle down, lad. Your da wants to keep you safe from harm. This is a seriously dangerous situation," Sean said, patiently.

I glanced into the room to find Broly and Needles waiting for Tommy. They peered up from their chairs and flipped me off.

"Just wait here with your mates and your da will

meet with you soon," Sean explained, calmly.

"What's with all these men out there?" I asked.

Sean grabbed my sleeve and pulled me lower to whisper.

"Things are in shambles. It's just terrible," Sean said.

We slowly crept into the office and I heard the yelling as we entered. Mulligan was infuriated. He held a crumpled paper in his hand, while he shouted into a mobile phone. Mulligan's face was red and sweaty, with veins protruding from his neck and forehead. "I don't fucking care. You find them. Do you hear me? Or you'll be the one they find dead!"

He threw the phone against the wall with a loud grunt. It shattered into several pieces onto to the floor.

"They've taken Anna!" Mulligan yelled, and mopped sweat from his forehead with a white handkerchief.

"I'm so sorry, sir. Who did this?"

"The Russians. The Gallaghers. They're all in it together. They want the goods back and - get this - they want you to deliver them. Here, see it for yourself. It says the American."

He threw the crumpled page in my direction. It bounced off my chest and landed at me feet. I picked it up and read that they were, in fact, demanding me.

"Black vans have been following me everywhere," I said.

Mulligan grabbed a bottle of Bushmills Black Irish whiskey, poured it into a glass, and gulped it down. He took another fast gulp and coughed.

"The garage got wrecked. Didn't they tell you? I just put down two of them in Dublin," I explained.

"That means we have a tout in our mist. I'll deal with that later. For now you're going over to Gallagher's place," Mulligan said.

"Can a few of those boys out there come along?" I asked.

"No."

"No?" I asked.

Just Danny will go. Get him," Mulligan said to Sean, who nodded and darted out.

"You won't need anyone else," he said.

Tommy must've been listening. He busted into

Mulligan's office desperate to help and win back his father's confidence.

"Da, me and me mates are coming along to help Danny. We can beat those fuckers down with the best of them." Tommy boasted.

"Get back out there. I'll call for you when I'm good and ready," Mulligan barked.

"But, da… I can do this," Tommy pleaded.

"No. This is a delicate situation, lad. They've given us specific instructions. The less people involved the better," Mulligan replied, showing a brief moment of patience.

Tommy shrank out of the office with a sigh and rejoined his anxious posse.

Sean returned with a grisly man with no neck and tree trunk legs, a colossal man in his late sixties who towered over me at about six and a half feet tall. His head was shaved with gray stubble on the sides and his hands were the size of melons. He also had a huge stomach, which was tucked into a dark green T-shirt that hung over his belt and blue jeans.

"Bill, this is Danny Murphy," Mulligan said.

"Great to meet you," I said.

"Don't let anything happen to Bill," Mulligan ordered.

Murphy stood a full head taller than Mulligan and wore a simpleton's expression while Mulligan addressed him.

"Is that understood?" Mulligan asked.

"Yes Mr. Mulligan," Danny said.

We shook hands and Danny's grip was firm, but gentle.

"Nice to meet you," I said.

"Right," Murphy said, and stared at me for a few awkward seconds.

"Now go out front and wait while Bill and I chat. We have some unfinished business," Mulligan said.

"Alright sir," Murphy said, and obeyed the order.

"Listen to me, Bill," Mulligan said once Murphy left. He walked over to his desk and poured more whiskey. "This is what they want, give it to them."

Mulligan took a big gulp and let out a hiss as he reached behind his desk and pulled out two large black suitcases. He laid one on top of his desk and then unclasped the locks. Inside the case were the bricks of white powder that I had taken from the warehouse.

"Take these valises to the Gallaghers, and don't come back without my Anna."

"Understood."

"One other thing, Bill. Danny may look simple, but he's sharp as a whip and has a violent temper. If he loses it just stay out of his way until he's finished."

I gave him a quizzical glance and he took another gulp of the whiskey. "Finished with what?"

"You'll see. Don't let me down Bill. I'm counting on you."

I walked out of Mulligan's office, through the noisy room of thugs, and headed out the front door. The snow had let up and Danny stood facing the front, hands in his pockets. I knew he was larger than me, but I didn't realize by how much until I walked up behind him.

He turned and pulled out a set of keys. "Are we all set?" I nodded. "I'll drive," he blurted, and we headed towards the gate.

Danny towered over the thugs guarding the gate.

He stepped within inches of one of the guards and glared down at him.

"Well? Hurry the fuck up and open it!" Danny barked.

Spit flew from Danny's mouth onto the guard's face. He just took a step back and opened the gate.

I followed Danny to a nineteen-nineties gunmetal gray Jaguar sedan.

I adjusted the gun from the back of my waistband before getting in. Murphy glanced at me and smiled.

"You won't be needing that."

CHAPTER TWENTY-NINE

Thirty minutes later we arrived at the Gallaghers' warehouse. To my surprise, all the damage had already been repaired. A few cars were parked in the fenced lot, but there didn't appear to be any goons or nefarious activity going on.

Danny pulled up to the loading dock and climbed out of the car. He never turned to see if I was following, then simply stomped up the stairs and through the main door of the warehouse. I quickened my pace to keep up and entered a few steps behind him.

The warehouse was brightly lit, with large crates piled high that were well organized and neat. We followed a series of signs that brought us to the main office, but still didn't see a soul. A gray door with the words "Main Office" painted in red was slightly ajar. I turned to Danny, and with a nod, he folded his arms and stood watch.

I peeked into the office. Fluorescent lights twitched, which gave the room a bluish tint with a slight strobe light effect as they pulsed. A guy who looked to be about eighty sat at a desk reading a newspaper, a lit cigarette in his hand. A black ashtray sat on the right edge of the desk, out of reach, but the old man clearly had no desire to use it as a long ash fell and litter the desk. He had disheveled white hair and wore a wrinkled plaid brown blazer. His mouth hung open with a dull expression as he scanned the newspaper unaware of my presence.

"Excuse me, Mr. Gallagher? I'm here to discuss the return of Anna Mulligan." He didn't look up or acknowledge me in any way.

"Excuse me, sir?" I tried again and stepped closer.

"He can't hear you."

A voice, deep and smooth, came from a dark corner.

"Who are you?" I asked.

"I'm Paul Gallagher. This is my office. That's my da. He lost his hearing a few years ago."

"Where's the girl?" I asked.

"We'll get to that shortly."

Paul Gallagher was a lean man in his fifties with graying hair and a pointy goatee. He sat legs crossed, smoking a cigarette. He took a long drag and let the smoke out slowly. The smoke hung around his head, which gave him a smoldering appearance.

"I brought your junk," I said.

"I see that. It's a good first step, but unfortunately it's not mine. The junk belongs to my business associates."

"So they have Mulligan's daughter?" I asked.

"We have a misunderstanding. I'm a businessman and I put my efforts where the money is. Your employer chooses to ignore opportunities I've placed right under his nose that could benefit all of us. I've reached out to Mulligan many times to create a partnership, but sadly, he refuses."

"So, stealing his trucks and kidnapping his daughter is good for business?"

"No, but I'm a man of action and clearly my message has now been received. The message is either you do business with us or face dire consequences. We are part of a large organization based in Eastern Europe. Our corporation will do whatever is necessary to control our interests in guns, and drug and sex trafficking. If I can't deliver, I too will be replaced. My associates have less patience with each passing day." He took a long drag on his cigarette. "Maybe you could convince Mulligan that it's in his best interest to comply. He trusts you and will listen. All this blood is bad for business."

Gallagher stroked his goatee, eyed me for a few beats, and slipped into thought. Seconds passed slowly as he twisted his gray beard into a point. He stood, stubbed out his cigarette, and stepped closer.

"Mulligan is very proud. I don't see him doing business with people who've threatened his family," I said.

"It's very simple. You make him understand or I'll be forced to deliver you to my associates."

Gallagher gave me a hard stare and sat back down. He reached into his shirt pocket, pulled out a silver cigarette case, and lit up another cigarette.

"Me? What are you talking about?" I asked.

"You're that American guy on the run? We know about you. The world is a very small place at times. You're a wanted man, Mr. O'Brien. Or is it Conlin? Either way, my associates will pay handsomely for your delivery. Dead or alive." He trailed off and went silent for a moment.

"There's been enough blood between us, so just make the deal with Mulligan and get him to join us."

"I can't do that. He won't listen."

"Oh, but you will. Your life depends on it," Gallagher hissed. He took another deep drag on his cigarette and the tip glowed red hot with a slight sizzle as the paper burned down the side.

"Make your own fucking deal with Mulligan. I'm moving on. This has nothing to do with me. Here, take your shit and I'm out."

I slammed the cases on the desk. Gallagher moved over to the desk, opened the cases, and nodded. He slipped an old mobile flip phone out of his pants pocket, opened it, and dialed. I stared bewildered at the old phone as he held it to his ear and spoke.

I stood and listened to the one sided conversation,

trying to read between the lines. Whatever was going on I didn't have much time.

"Hey, yeah he's here. Yes, he brought it. Fine, I'll tell him. Bye." Gallagher ended the call and gave me a side-glance.

"Here is my card. Give it to Mulligan and tell him to call me tonight. Let him know that this could be a great business venture that would make us all very rich. There's plenty of money to share.

The office door flung open and a man pushed Anna into my arms. She appeared physically unharmed, but hysterical from her ordeal she sobbed uncontrollably. I put my jacket around her shoulders and held her.

"Shush. You're okay now, we're going home."

"Oh, thank God you're here." She burst into tears. Anna hugged herself nervously, trying to calm down as she took a few shuttering breaths.

"Remember my words, Bill. Convince Mulligan or you'll be heading to Eastern Europe in a box. Now you are both free to go."

A loud crash broke the uncomfortable silence as

something heavy slammed against the office door and shook the walls. We rushed out to see a thin looking man with greasy long dark hair, and a crowbar yelling from on top a group of crates. He shouted orders at five thugs that surrounded Danny Murphy.

"C'mon Grandpa, let's see what you got."

Danny stood still, arms folded. They lunged at him, but Danny moved with speed and precision, using what appeared to be a combination of martial arts as he sidestepped the first attacker. Danny then took him by the arm and swung him around. The flying man's feet collided with the face of another thug and Danny released him, crashing into a group of wooden crates where he lay unconscious. The other thugs attacked Danny and he took them all down, one by one.

Grab, swing and release. The thugs flew across the warehouse in different directions and smashed into crates until no one was left conscious.

The junkie-looking leader continued to yell and curse at his fallen henchmen, but no one responded. Desperation overtook him and he jumped down off the crates and swung the crowbar wildly at Danny. He came in with awkward swipes and cursed at the top of his lungs.

"Terry, no. Stop!" Paul Gallagher roared and pushed past me, but it was too late.

Terry rushed in, eyes wide, with a half dozen wild swings, and Danny blocked Terry's arm. It broke with a sickening snap. The crowbar clattered to the floor and Paul Gallagher ran over to his brother, who had collapsed to the floor clutching his arm. Terry's arm lay bent at an unnatural angle as he moaned in pain.

Danny walked over to Paul who cradled his broken brother.

"Paul, you really should get your brother into rehab before he hurts himself. C'mon Bill, let's get Anna in the car," Danny said, and walked away.

CHAPTER THIRTY

The car ride back was quiet except for Anna's quiet sobs. Danny didn't say anything and I spent the time reliving the smooth words of Paul Gallagher and the actions of Danny Murphy. That sound of breaking bone echoed in the back of my mind and turned my stomach. I could still picture Terry Gallagher's arm hanging at a sickening angle.

Paul Gallagher knew all about my checkered past. Associates from Eastern European were searching for me? Who were they? Had Viktor put a contract out on me? I didn't know, but my time here was finished. With or without Mulligan's help I had to leave Ireland and regroup with Yuri.

I had serious doubts that Mulligan would do any business with Gallagher or his associates, and a war surely was looming, but I knew whatever the outcome I had been compromised.

We arrived at Mulligan's farm, with the cars and security still in place. I climbed out of the Jaguar and a blast of freezing air instantly snapped me out of my thoughts. I opened the rear car door and helped Anna out of the backseat. I put my arm around her and we followed Danny towards the house. The sentries opened the gate and quickly stepped out of Danny's way without a word.

When we got to Mulligan's office, Danny knocked on the closed door and immediately it swung open. Mulligan bolted out and grabbed Anna in a tender embrace.

Oh, my poor girl. I'm so sorry you had to go through this. Are you alright? Did they hurt you?"

"A little when they grabbed me. I didn't know what this was about and that frightened me."

They walked into Mulligan's office and closed the door.

Danny and I stepped into the living room to give them some time. After a while Mulligan sent Sean to retrieve us and he greeted us with a huge grin. Mulligan rushed over and hugged Danny. Then rushed me and squeezed me in the same kind of enthusiastic hug, lifting me off the ground and letting me drop.

"You did it. I knew it. Me girl's safely home. Aww it's a big day indeed, lads."

Mulligan poured Irish whiskey into three glasses.

"Umm... Mr. Mulligan, we delivered the brief cases, but there was a slight problem. A crew of Gallagher thugs jumped us, but Danny took care of it.

"Of course he did." Mulligan beamed.

He waved his hand and shook his head to dismiss any need to worry. Then he handed Danny and I whiskeys and clinked the glasses hard. We all downed the whiskey and he poured more.

"There's some unfinished business, Mr. Mulligan," I said, still tasting the whiskey as I spoke.

"There is? What business? Only killing those pesky Gallaghers," he said, with a throaty laugh.

"Sir, I have a message from Paul Gallagher."

"Oh yeah, what's that?" Mulligan asked.

"He wants to form a partnership or he's going to kill me. Here's his card." I placed the card on his desk.

"I'm all for being mates and neighborly, now aye? Let's ring him and see."

He pulled a mobile phone from his pants pocket and punched in the number from the card. Mulligan winked at me with a smile and a nod as he held the phone to his ear.

"Paul? This is Doyle. My man here tells me we're new business partners. Yeah, you've said that before. He did? Oh, that is unfortunate. Well, I hope your brother feels better soon."

He picked up the bottle and poured three fingers into his glass. He took a long, slow sip and winked at me.

"Right, double my profits? Okay, brilliant. When will I meet your new friends? I see. Sounds good. Keep your pecker up and talk to you soon." Mulligan closed the phone and took a large gulp of the whiskey.

"That went surprisingly well, sir. I didn't think you'd even speak to him."

"Well, me boyo, I'll let you in on a little secret." He poured more whiskey into his glass and knocked it back. "Chief Gerry is heading over there as we speak to bust those fuckers. A crew of Garda carrying Hurleys will crack their heads open. Those Gallagher boys are gonna do hard time. They might even run into a little accident. I understand that jail can be a rough place," Mulligan said.

"You outsmarted them, sir, but what about Gallagher's partners?" I asked.

"Yes, I'm putting them out of business too. It's over, laddie."

Mulligan went into a file cabinet and handed me another thick white envelope. I peeked inside and found about twenty thousand euros.

"This is extremely generous, sir."

"What's this? You're not drinking. This is a celebration son, drink up!" Mulligan said.

He poured more whiskey into my empty glass and I shot it back. It went down easier this time, smooth and warming. I now had enough cash to leave Ireland.

"Mr. Mulligan, I hope it's okay if I move on now?" I   asked.

"Of course. You've done me a great service. Sean will help you with whatever you need. Just be at Tommy's boxing match Friday night. We'll have our last celebration before you go.," he said.

"Friday?" I accidentally said aloud.

I felt a pang of sadness at the thought of telling Janette about my departure. She was the best thing in my life, but I could feel my hatred for Viktor still burning inside me.

"That's right, Bill. Today is Wednesday and then comes Thursday and Friday. Are you okay? Did you get hit in the head?" He glanced over at Danny and shrugged. "You'd better get going. I've got to meet with Chief Gerry and pick up my cases."

He poured more whiskey into the three glasses and held up his glass for one last toast.

"Here's to Tommy's big win Friday," Mulligan cheered.

I shot back the whiskey and stood up to leave.

"Thank you, sir." I held up the envelope and stepped towards the door.

"Remember, Bill, if you need anything for your trip east, contact Sean. I've told him to set you up.

"That'll be helpful, sir."

I headed down the hallway when I heard Mulligan call me back. I stuck my head back in his office.

"Yes sir?"

"You won't be seeing Morris again. He was on Gallagher's payroll, that fucking tout."

"Morris? He spoke so fondly of you. How did you decide on him?"

"Who else would be giving out car info on you, boyo? Anyway it's done," he said, and furrowed his brow.

"I'll see you at the fight."

Mulligan's phone buzzed and he answered it. "Alright Chief. It's all taken care of? It is? That's brilliant. When will you be bringing me case back? I'll be needing it straight away," Mulligan said.

He waved me out. I turned, nodded good-bye to Danny, and shook his hand.

"Thanks, Danny. See you around."

"Take care of yourself, Bill."

I walked down the hallway with Morris' betrayal weighing heavily on me. How could it have been Morris? This had to have been a horrible mistake. I went into the big living room and noticed it had cleared out. A few guys were still talking and drinking. I found Sean chatting it up with a couple of burly looking men. He smiled and struggled to lift his head, but seemed to be enjoying the conversation.

I wondered how he could be laughing when Morris was dead. I thought they were friends. Poor Morris was probably tortured for information about the Gallagher's operations. Who knew if he even knew anything? I got the connection to the cars, but it seemed too easy. He was such a nice regular guy. How did Mulligan figure it out?

I walked up close to Sean and pulled him aside by the arm. He looked down at my hand gripping his upper arm and took a step back.

"What happened to Morris? I thought you were tight as family," I asked.

"Well, we were, but our business tends to get in the way sometimes. He wasn't loyal or careful. Being a tout is the worst thing of all. We take that seriously and I had to turn him in."

"How can you be so casual about what they did to

him?" I asked.

"Look, Bill, I know it's hard to understand, but he could've gotten us all killed because of his greed. You were hunted and almost kill because of his actions. The chess game is over and Doyle's won. He's just better at it then the Gallaghers. C'mon let's go, I'll give you a lift into town."

He patted my back and pushed me towards the front door. "It'll all be better now. You've done a great job and can move on."

I stepped outside, lit up a cig, and blew the smoke out hard. I turned to Sean. "How did you know it was Morris?"

"It was that damn car of his. How could the whole shop be destroyed except the love of his life? That old piece of shit killed him," Sean said.

Most of the cars that had been jammed the driveway and street were gone. I got into Sean's car and we left. I couldn't help but wonder if it really was Morris. It felt wrong, like a setup.

I asked Sean to drop me off at the Red Lion. We sat in an uncomfortable silence until we entered the outskirts of Dublin.

"You know the chances are pretty good that this is not over," I said.

"Those Gallagher boy will die in jail before causing any more trouble."

"I doubt it."

"Why's that?" Sean asked.

"All it takes is one call to Gallagher's associates and we'll have a war on our hands. Paul Gallagher mentioned slipping information about my whereabouts to people that want me dead. What's to say he didn't also drop a message about Mr. Mulligan before all this went down?"

"Doyle and Chief Gerry have this all buttoned up. They won't be making any phone calls. Just get your own affairs in order," Sean said. The car abruptly stopped. "I've had enough of you. Get out," he said.

"Okay, I get it, but Gallagher's connection are not just a small crew of local thugs. There's a never-ending supply of goons from Russia."

I got out and Sean skidded away from the curb. The tires kicked up gravel and dirt as the car took off.

I hadn't even had a chance to shut the door.

There was something very wrong with Sean. Mind my own business? Not likely, but it was weird. No one in Mulligan's crew was concerned about any fallout or going up against the Russians. They weren't even interested in being prepared.

A chill ran through me as goose flesh raised the hair on my arms. I zipped up my coat, turned up the collar, and walked towards town. Cars zipped passed me, their red taillights trailed like streaks of paint on a shadowy gray background. It was probably a couple of miles into the heart of Dublin. I pulled out my hard pack of reds and lit one up. My lighter glowed like a beacon in the darkening dusk. I blew out the smoke and took in the cool air, clean and sobering. I puffed, walked and listened to the rhythm of my boots as they scrapped along the dark asphalt.

What was it Sean said? "Get *my* affairs in order." Isn't that what they say before someone dies? Maybe I was just being paranoid.

CHAPTER THIRTY-ONE

My walk into town was uneventful. When I got closer to Dublin I sent Janette a text to let her know I was coming over. Her response was a simple *k*. About an hour later I'd finished half a pack of cigs and arrived sweaty and overheated at Janette's flat. I rang the buzzer and waited for her to let me in.

"Yeah. Who is it?"

"It's me."

"You're still alive? That's great."

"Yup still kicking."

Janette buzzed the front door open, and I pushed my way in. I took one last glance of the street. It was empty and eerily silent. I walked down the hallway not really paying much attention and wondered how to best tell Janette that I had to leave. I approached apartment three and I looked up, Janette peeked out of the door.

"That good huh?"

"Sorry, I've got a lot on my mind."

She grabbed my jacket and pulled me into the apartment with a hard kiss. Her lips were warm and she slammed the door shut behind us.

"Want a beer?"

"Sure."

I took my coat off, hung it on the back of the chair, and sat at her counter. She handed me a cold beer and I took a few gulps before I realized just how thirsty I was.

"My boss' son is fighting Friday night and he gave me these."

I pulled out the tickets to show her.

"He wants me there. Wanna go?" I slid the tickets across the counter.

"Is that it? That's the best you can do for a Friday night date. Weak," she said, with a pout.

"Well, I'm sure we can find some other stuff to do," I said, and lifted my eyebrows.

She frowned at me, unimpressed.

"I mean we'll go someplace nice for… dinner and

drinks," I said, and adjusted my lame pitch.

"That's a little better. I don't know, it depends," she said.

"Depends on what?" I asked.

"Your performance tonight," she said, with a smirk and disappeared into the bedroom.

I finished my beer, and then took a scalding shower, washing with speed and purpose. When I entered Janette's bedroom and she was standing against the wall in a white silk robe. Her nipples were hard and clearly defined underneath the shear material. I stepped closer and touched her body through the robe. Our eyes locked and I drew her closer for a kiss.

"No," she said, and pushed me down on the bed. She then went back over to her dresser and plugged her phone into a radio. Soft music filled the room.

Slowly she began to move her hips to the rhythm. She opened and closed her robe and teased me with her body. Her erotic dance drove me crazy. I could hardly control myself and crawled off the bed. I pulled her close for a passionate kiss. I was hot with desire and her mouth only made me more impatient.

"I said no," she barked, and shoved me back on the bed.

"What a tease, c'mon. Get over here."

"Hang in on lover man, it'll be worth it."

She gave me a shy smile and went back to her dance. Then let the robe drop to the floor. Janette danced in just her panties and slowly touched her breasts and swayed slowly to the music. I sat back and took in her beauty. I desperately needed to feel her body and I was starving for her touch. She shut the light and crawled onto the edge of bed and pulled off my pants. I put my hands on her face and pulled her to my mouth. We collided in a desperate embrace of passion and hunger. She blew softly against my neck as I entered her. Our bodies discovered the same rhythm until we both finished in a wet quivering orgasm. I feel fast asleep, warm, fuzzy, and quenched.

Hours later Janette shook me awake.

"Did you hear that?" she whispered, panic in her voice.

"What?" I asked, and tried to shake myself awake.

I heard a scratching sound and shot out of bed to investigate. It was definitely coming from one of the windows. I leaned up against the wall and peeked out of the bedroom window. A man dressed in black with a mask was on the fire escape. Another sound came from the living room and I knew we were in trouble.

Where did I leave my gun?

A dozy cloud clogged my mind, but I remembered it was in the bathroom when I showered. I rushed in and grabbed my Beretta 9mm. A loud shattering of glass broke the silence and Janette screamed. She rushed into the bathroom shaking.

"What are you gonna do?" she asked, squeezing my arm.

"Lock yourself in here," I said. I shoved her in and closed the door.

"No, I can help."

"You'll get in the way," I barked, and slammed the door shut.

I turned to face the intruders. A large man with a baklava climbed through the window. His boots crunched loudly on broken shards of glass. I could barely make out his form in the darkness, but I saw light reflect off the shape of a gun. He raised his arm with his pistol out front and I fired three quick bursts into his torso. Fire flashed from the gun's muzzle and lit up the room like a strobe light. He crumpled to the floor with a loud grunt and his gun clattered into the darkness.

Without warning a black blur hit my arm and the pain made me lose control of my hand. The intruder slammed me against the wall and my gun skidded out of reach. The first intruder was dead and the second alive and on top of me, my odds were getting slightly better.

He rained punches down on my head, but I held up my forearms for protection. Quickly he sat on my chest and pinned my arms. I bucked him off and scrambled in a crab walk to the bedroom. He clawed and scratched at my legs, but I was too fast and had just enough time to turn and swing wildly at his head. He came in low, tackled me, and we tumbled onto the bed. I rolled off and rushed back in to grab him, but tripped over the dead guy. I went down and he was immediately on top. I panicked and tried desperately to gain control, but he had me out-positioned. His hands were around my throat and he squeezed down hard, cutting off my air.

I tore at his mask and tried to block his airflow, but it was useless. I was out of breath and couldn't release his hold. Dark spots quickly clouded my vision until I blacked out.

I came to and gasped for air. The last the thing I recalled was the acrid stench of sour sweat and hands around my throat like a vise. I took in small amounts air and coughed uncontrollably. My lungs burned as I struggled to breathe. A string of spittle dripped onto the floor and I stared at nothing trying to regain my composure and propped myself up, but collapsed. The room suddenly dropped and spun, as my head throbbed with pain and confusion.

Things slowly resolved and off in the distance I heard the cries of a woman. I blinked and wheezed as the room slowly came back into focus. Janette shook my shoulder and shouted, but I couldn't understand what she was saying. She sat on her knees, face soaked with tears.

"Bill, Bill wake up."

Rivulets of tears ran down her cheeks and dripped off her chin.

"What happened?" I asked.

I sat up and wiped the spit from my mouth. The second intruder lay dead on Janette's bed. Half his head was missing from a gapping wound. He lay at an odd angle, blood and gore covered the walls and pooled on the sheets.

Janette wailed in shock, horrified by what she'd done, but she saved my life. I tried to make sense of the scene and calm her down. On the floor next to her lay my Beretta 9mm.

"I heard a big crash and then everything went quiet. I peeked out and saw this large guy choking you so I picked up your gun and pulled the trigger until he stopped. It was horrible, his head exploded like a melon all over the wall."

"You saved my life. Do you have any other blankets?" I asked.

"Yes," she replied, but didn't move.

"Janette? We need to wrap these guys up," I said, but she couldn't hear me.

"Janette, it's going to be alright.

"How? How could this ever be alright?"

"I know you've been through a lot, but you can get through this. C'mon let's get out of this room."

I helped her into the living room and called Mulligan.

"What is it?" he asked in a scratchy voice.

"Sorry to call so late, sir, but I have a situation. Do you have a cleaning crew?"

I gave him Janette's address.

"It'll all be taken care of and I'll call Chief Gerry in case any busy bodies call it in. You can fill me in on Friday. You are still coming to see Tommy, right?" Mulligan asked, just like it was another day at the office.

"Yes I'm still coming."

"Brilliant," Mulligan said, and ended the call.

Thirty minutes later a knock came to the door. I looked through the peephole and saw a weathered old man with a long gray beard wearing a cap.

"Who is it?" I asked.

"What? Are ye daft? Doyle sent us. Hurry up and open the door, before we leave," he said, gruffly.

I opened the door and they pushed past me. Three short old timers with boozy breath. They rolled in with two dollies, a mop and pail, a box of industrial contractor green plastic bags, and disinfectant spray bottles.

They looked oddly like identical triplets and they were. Their clothes the only way to tell them apart. One wore a dark red sweater, the other a black sweater and the third had a green plaid collared shirt. They reeked of mothballs and also whiskey and smoke like they had come here straight from a bar. The combination was so nasty that it immediately saturated Janette's flat.

"You boys out drinking tonight?" I asked.

"What are you my wife?" Red Sweater growled.

"No, you got that wrong. He's my AA sponsor. You know one step at a time," Green Plaid said.

"You mean one day at a time and twelve steps, you Egit," Black Sweater said.

"Hey, take it easy," I said.

These crusty triplets were nothing like the professional cleaners back in New York, but it was all I had. Two of the brothers put the bodies and blankets into the large dark green contractor bags, while the other mopped up the bloody bits. They wrapped everything in duct tape and wheeled the bodies towards the door. It was oddly comical. I couldn't believe they'd never been arrested.

"Mulligan should really retire these old bastards and get some modern cleaners," I said, but Janette didn't respond.

I glanced over at Janette. She sat on the couch wrapped in a blanket and stared out the window, eyes wide in shock.

Her eyes slowly shifted towards me. She stood to face me and let the blanket slipped off her shoulders to the floor.

"I want my own gun. Get me one."

CHAPTER THIRTY-TWO

It was just dumb luck that the Gallaghers survived their short time in jail and Chief Gerry was unable to close any deal on silencing them. Interpol agents were somehow alerted and arrived immediately after their capture to release them. It seemed fishy that anyone would care, but the Gallaghers must've had strong connections across the board. They were quickly plucked up with a convoy of black vans to an unknown location. The big money on the line could easily corrupt any public or agency official.

I couldn't help but feel things getting more complicated. I had a ton of questions about Mulligan, the Russians and now that Interpol was involved I had a dark suspicion that the FBI wouldn't be far behind. I didn't have much time left and this unnerved me.

I surprised Janette with a Browning .22 caliber pistol, but the disappointment on her face was unmistakable. She laughed in my face and told me to get her a real gun. However, she still took the .22 and put it in her drawer under her panties as a backup. We compromised on a subcompact Glock 45, which was able to fit in her purse and could still blow a baseball size hole through anyone.

We woke up early and went to a shooting range just outside of Dublin, within a few hours Janette had become more comfortable, confident and pretty good at hitting the targets. By Friday, we were closer than ever before.

Janette and I were having drinks in her apartment on Friday when my phone buzzed in my pocket. I looked down and saw Sean's name.

"Hey Sean."

"Bill, Doyle wants everyone to meet a little early at the gym. Can you come by now?" he asked.

"Sure, I'm on my way."

Janette gave me a hard look as I ended the call.

"What's this about Bill?"

"I have to go to a meeting before the fight."

"Let's go."

"I don't think that's a good idea," I said.

"Why not? I have a gun now too."

"These are dangerous people, I want you safe."

"How safe am I in my own flat?"

"Good point."

We went outside into the chilly night. I expected cold rain, but snowflakes floated came down like confetti and coated everything, which transformed the gray city into a beautiful white quaint town. I zipped up my jacket and lit a cig. Janette clutched her coat closed around her neck and paced as she shivered and searched the street for an available taxi.

"I still don't think this is a good idea you coming along," I said.

"Well, too bad. You're not leaving me alone with all this shit going on."

"This is taking too long. I have to get to the gym. Don't you have a taxi service number we can call?" I hissed.

Just then a dark navy car pulled to the curb. The driver rolled down his window. "Where are you folks headed?"

"Mulligan's Boxing Gym in Blackrock," I said.

"Well hop on in."

We climbed into the backseat and the driver took off.

"I'll get you there straight away. Heading to the big fight, aye. I've heard all about it. Should be a fine fight."

We were on the southern outskirts of Dublin when red-flashing lights came up fast behind us. I thought they were going to pass us, but they forced the taxi to the shoulder. Janette and I were thrown to the side and jolted forward as the driver swerved to avoid hitting the police car and slammed on his breaks. He stopped abruptly inches from the guardrail. In seconds another car pulled behind and boxed us in.

To my disbelief Chief Gerry got out of the car in front of us. He stepped over, tapped on the window and signaled the driver to roll it down. I turned around to see another constable on the left side. He stood a few feet back with a gun in his hand. I had a bad feeling about this.

"Hey Chief. Is everything okay? Did something happen?" I asked.

"Shut your hole. Put your hands up and step out

one at a time." Chief Gerry ordered.

"What's this about sir? I don't understand," the driver said.

"You have a very dangerous passenger in your taxi tonight. He's wanted for several murders here and in America. Please step out of the vehicle now and no funny business. That goes for you too, miss."

Carefully we got out of the backseat. I led the way out, my hands held high. Chief Gerry violently pushed me down on the car hood and patted me down. The other constable asked Janette to sit down on the curb and watched her while I was searched.

"Oh ho, what's this?" Chief Gerry said, and held up my Beretta 9mm.

At that second I launched into action and swept out his legs. He awkwardly fell backwards on the pavement. The Beretta flew a few feet away and skidded into the grass. I rushed in and jumped on top of him with a series of head butts to his face. I heard a sickening crack as dark red blood flowed from his nose, his eyes rolled back in his head and he passed out.

I turned to fight the other constable. "Run!" I yelled.

Janette took off. She hopped over the rail and into the woods. The other constable scurried over with his gun pointed at my face. I put my hands up and didn't resist. He didn't hesitate and swung the pistol smashing the side of my skull. A white flash of pain rattled my skull. Immediately all sound stopped and was replaced by a high-pitched whine that rang in my ears. I struggled to stay conscious and went to one knee, but another whack finished me off and I faded into a shadowy slumber.

CHAPTER THIRTY-THREE

My eyes felt crusty and sealed shut. I took a deep breath, forced them open and tried to figure out what had happened. I slowly remembered the encounter with Chief Gerry on the roadside and Janette's escape.

I realized that a jail cell would be my new home for a long time. I'd face years in jail on multiple murders charges and probably would be extradited to New York City.

From off in the distance I heard a raspy voice. It came closer and called my name.

"Bill. Bill. Can you hear me? C'mon lad, wake up."

A spike of pain shot through my skull so severe that a wave of nausea made me gag. I forced the bile back down and blacked out.

After a while, I awoke and tried to wipe my mouth, but my hands couldn't move. I pulled hard, but it was no use. My hands were cuffed behind me to the chair. I looked around. This was no jail. It was a dusty warehouse. An old man sat next to me also cuffed to his chair. His face swollen and bloody, with his chin on his chest. Gray hair hung over his face and blood had dripped all over his shirt from his injuries.

"Did I recognize him?" I considered his features.

Think.

Think.

The place didn't look familiar and silence filled my ears except for the sound of the old man next to me. His raspy breaths created a rhythm that I held onto for a few beats. I shook my head to get rid of the cobwebs, but a sharp ache shot through my right temple. I squeezed my eyes tight to suppress the agony as it spiked.

"Bill, are you alright? We have to get out of here."

I took another look at the old man. I knew him. It was Doyle Mulligan, bloodied, battered and with one eye swollen shut.

"What happened? What are we doing here? Are we under arrest?" I asked. Before he could answer I heard footsteps coming from outside the room. The door creaked open and Sean came in, with his hands behind his back in that bowed stance. He marched towards us hunched over with a gate of confidence, as if he was inspecting a prize or a special project. He struggled to lift his head, but with a side glance peered at us through his blunt haircut. Sean walked over to Doyle with a thin smirk.

"Doyle fucked up, Bill. He had a once in a lifetime opportunity and he blew it. Paul Gallagher and the Russians… Well you know… they needed a new partner and I can't let it pass. They'll pay well for the both of you. Doyle's too daft and stuck in his old ways to see the big picture. So, we took matters into our own hands."

"You're a fucking traitor," Doyle growled.

"Shut your mouth," Sean said, and swiftly smacked Doyle across the face with a pistol.

Doyle let out a grunt and winced in pain, but didn't respond.

"Wait a sec. We? What are you saying?" I demanded.

"Oh yes, you'll fetch a nice bounty too. You just love to piss off people wherever you go? These folks are willing to pay big for you. Just sit tight, the Russians will be here shortly to scoop you up and give me the bounty."

Sean walked out and closed the door behind him without another word.

"Doyle what happened? Why are you here?" I asked.

"Chief Gerry crossed me. Can't believe after all these years he'd do this over money. I went to pick up the white powder, but they had other plans for me."

"The Chief?" I asked, baffled.

"Yes."

"Chief Gerry came after me too, but it doesn't make any sense," I said.

"It doesn't have to make sense. Every man has a price." Mulligan sighed.

He spit out the words like bitter poison on his lips.

After a long while, I heard loud voices and heavy footsteps that echoed in the warehouse. A large group of men were headed towards us.

I blinked myself awake and called out to Doyle, but he didn't stir. The door swung open with aloud crash and bounced off the wall. A figure stood in the doorway. I tried to focus on the face, but he stayed in the shadows. I could feel his eyes on me. Was it the Chief? It didn't look like his body shape.

When he stepped closer a chill ran through me. I never expected to see Vlad the weasel again. I thought leaving his ship would've been enough to satisfy him, but I was wrong and he wanted revenge. The captain had warned me that I wasn't finished with Vlad. How could I have known that his connections could reach this deep into the Russian mob?

"We have some unfinished business. Mr. Big Apple," he hissed.

Four other men entered the room behind him. Two walked with limps and as they entered I quickly realized who they were. Their boots filled the room and I was paralyzed with fear. Now I knew who they were and what they wanted. I'd shot and crippled these goons in the bowels of the ship.

"Payback is a bitch," Vlad spit each word out slowly.

Vlad reached into his coat, revealed a black pistol and chambered a round. He pointed the gun at my knee, with an expression of pure satisfaction. It moved across his face and then slid away.

Vlad abruptly stopped as if awoken from a dream. His expression changed to a scowl and he turned to the henchmen behind him. They huddled for a few moments and then Vlad handed the gun to one of the limping goons.

"Here, you do it!" Vlad ordered, and handed him the gun.

He stepped forward and pressed the gun hard into my knee. I gasped from the pressure of the gun against my bones.

"This is just the first bullet friend," he growled, with a gleeful smile.

I took a deep breath and held it with my eyes squeezed tight in anticipation.

Suddenly, a loud explosion sounded with an impact so strong that the floor shook. Everyone in the room jumped and turned in the direction of the blast. Doyle awoke and scanned the room with panic in his eyes.

He glared at me with a bewildered expression as another explosion rocked the building and was followed by the clatter of automatic weapons. The goons yelled in Russian and rapidly abandoned the office.

Beads of sweat rolled down my forehead as I tried to catch my breath after that close call. This was my only chance and I needed to act quickly. I threw my head back several times until my chair tipped off balanced and crashed onto the ground. My head hit hard, a flash of pain cut through my head. I blinked frantically to stop from blacking out, my vision filled with stars, but I managed to hold onto my consciousness. I rolled over onto my knees, stood with the chair on my back. I smashed the back of the chair into the wall with everything I had. Again and again I rammed the chair until it grew weak. Each blow rippled through my body, but I hoped the chair would give up before me. My legs burned and began to shake uncontrollably with the effort. They felt like rubber as I ran out of steam. *C'mon, you have to do this,* I thought and pushed myself on.

I panted hard, my heart pounded at an odd beat from the exertion. I tried to catch my breath for a few seconds and then started again. I yelled out and gave it another big burst of energy into the wall. This time the chair legs splintered and broke apart with a loud crack. All I heard as I collapsed to the floor out of breath with my face soaked in sweat was Doyle's panicked cries to hurry. Still cuffed to the back of the chair and desperate to be free, I slid the chair back under my butt and past the backs of my legs. I held the broken seat like a shield and froze. Footsteps were coming this way and I needed to free Doyle. Frantically I searched the room, but found nothing to use. We desperately needed a key.

The gunfire in the warehouse continued, but footsteps still came this way. I pressed myself flat against the wall by the door jam. Salty sweat dripped into my eyes, which stung and blurred my vision.

The door snapped open and Sean shuffled in hunched over a gun in his hand. I slammed the chair back into the unsuspecting old man and knocked his gun away. It bounced across the room, but that didn't stop Sean. To my astonishment he somehow managed to produce a collapsible metal baton. He flicked his wrist and connected with the side of my skull. I went down hard on my side, with stars and spots in my vision. The air was forced out of my lungs and I gasped for air on the dusty wooden floor. Sean rushed in and pummeled me with his metal baton. He grunted and muttered to himself as his ferocious barrage pounded my arms and ribs.

"You're going to die. This is my chance, my dream you hear!" Sean shouted.

"Crush that back-stabbing traitor," Doyle urged, from his confinement.

I struggled to protect my head and regain my wits. Sean began to fade and his blows grew ever weaker. His last strikes had nothing behind them and I saw my opportunity. I kicked out his legs and he hit the ground with a wince of pain. The baton clattered away out of reach and I stood over him bruised and panting. He looked up unable to right himself and I cracked him with the chair back. Blood trickled from the side of his face and he collapsed in a lifeless heap.

I frantically searched Sean's pockets, found a set of keys and fumbled for the cuff key.

"C'mon Bill, hurry up!" Doyle pleaded. He yanked at his bounds, but the steel cuffs were too strong.

I came behind Doyle and unlocked his cuffs.

An unnerving silence filled the warehouse. No screams, explosions or gunfire. We froze, looked at each other and Doyle rushed to unlock my cuffs. Our time ran out as the door handle turned. I picked up a broken chair leg to use as a weapon. I could only imagine what we looked like as a strike force, bloody and beaten, with broken furniture in our hands.

Doyle grabbed Sean's feet and pulled his dead body away from the doorway. The silence was disturbed by the creak of the office door and I leaned back against the wall and watched as it slowly opened. Doyle pressed himself against the wall on the other side with a chair leg in his hand. He gave me a hard glare and nodded, we were as ready as we'd ever be. I took a deep breath and held it ready to attack the first person that entered.

Doyle's expression completely changed as he

recognized the person at the door and dropped his chair leg. His face transformed from a grimace to a relaxed gap and then a smile. I couldn't see who it was, but whatever was going on Doyle's face said it all. A giant man stepped into the room. Danny Murphy had rescued us.

"They've all run off," he said.

"Oh praise the saints. You scared the bejesus outta me," Doyle said.

"Are you alright sir?" Danny asked.

"Alright? No, but I'll be great once we're outta here. But how did you find us?" Doyle asked, amazed.

"It was Bill's friend. You've got a special lady there, boyo. She came rushing down to the gym and told us what happened and who called Bill for the meeting. It was easy to figure it out from there. You'd better hold onto that one. She's got sand mate." Danny said.

"Where'd the rest go?" I asked.

"Dead or on the run."

"I brought a few of the boys with me. Once their numbers started to thin out, the survivors jumped in a van and took off. We'd better wrap this up," Danny said.

"Did you see a ferret looking guy with them?" I asked.

"No, I was too busy thinning their numbers. Word on the street is that Chief Gerry took a nice stack of cash from the Gallaghers. The Russians are set to take over your operation, Doyle."

"We'll see about that. I won't go down easy. They'll have to choke on my bones before swallowing me up," Doyle snarled.

The color came back into his cheeks as his anger rose.

"A few days after we busted up Gallagher's place, that half wit Terry started throwing money around at some Russian club. I think it's called Prague," Danny said.

"No it's Pravda," I said.

"Go put these rabid dogs down." Doyle ordered.

Rage on his face, he turned and spit on Sean's corpse.

"Better yet I'm coming too." Doyle growled.

Bodies and blood littered Doyle's warehouse floor,

which Sean managed. It looked as if a tornado had busted through the shattered and splintered front entrance. Doyle's crew had taken heavy losses, but so did the Russians and in the end Danny had led a successful rescue. I found two of Vlad's men sprawled out motionless and full of holes, guns still in their hands with blank dead faces.

Doyle stumbled outside of his warehouse, eyes wide with pure rage, he through his head back and screamed at the night sky. We got into Danny's car and he drove off to the club with three carloads of armed men in our motorcade.

CHAPTER THIRTY-FOUR

When we arrived at Club Pravda I glanced down at my phone. The time was nearly 3am. The club was still buzzing with activity. The parking lot was full of cars with a line of customers out front who had no idea of the approaching brigade.

Two hulking bouncers stood by the entrance with headsets selecting customers for the last leg of the evening. The bouncers wore black leather jackets with bulging outlines of barely concealed weapons. A crowd formed a line that wrapped around the building and into the lot. Beautiful woman dolled up with heavy make-up and short dresses with high heels lined up with slick men studded out in dark suites. They tried to get in, but even in New York it was always difficult to get the bouncers attention for a chance to drink and dance before closing. It was a busy Friday night and business was extremely good, but things were about to get real ugly.

Danny Murphy drove past the front and into the back of the parking lot. I scanned the entrance and looked for any signs of trouble, but found none. He parked and abruptly jumped out with a sense of determination and went around the back popping open the trunk. I followed him to the trunk and found an arsenal of weapons. I grabbed a M27 rifle, a couple of magazines and headed for the front door. The rest of the crew climb out of their cars and loaded up with a series of metal clicks readied their weapons.

Danny marched with single-mindedness to the front door weaving between parked cars. As we approached a group of armed men popped out of cars near the entrance and opened fire. Bullets ricocheted off the cars in a burst of pings and sparks. I tapped the trigger of the M27 and returned fire at the front line of defenders. The crowd screamed and dispersed from the uproar of gunfire.

Vlad popped out of one of the cars, ducked his head down low, and bolted into the club. I ran around the side to flank the action and identified the position of the men shooting at Danny's crew. One thug hurried to the back seat of his car and emerged with a rocket launcher. He quickly loaded a rocket into the launcher unaware that I had come around to his side. The M27 I was using didn't have the scope so I aimed down the iron sights. I closed one eye, took a deep breath, let it out slowly and fired a short burst. The muzzle flashed in the darkness, as one of my bullets hit the rocket and a glaring hot fireball erupted. The heat blasted my face as I ducked down behind a car for cover. The thug was completely disintegrated, cars cairned sideways and started a chain reaction of explosions from their gas tanks that shook the ground. I darted up again and picked off a couple defenders that held on, but others fled for the dark cover of the woods and quickly disappeared.

Danny's men chased down the few that sought shelter in the woods surrounding the parking lot. Flashes of gunfire lit up silhouetted trees in the darkness. The final defenders made their last stand in the tree line but were promptly put down.

I loaded another clip and moved quickly towards

the entrance. People frantically poured out of the main doors with panicked frightened faces and hands held high. Off in the distance the sounds of sirens floated on the breeze like an ominous warning and I knew our time was running out.

"C'mon Bill, we have to go!" Doyle shouted from Danny's car.

"I have to get that fucking weasel or this will never end!" I yelled.

Danny Murphy ran up besides me with a blood lust grin on his face.

"Let's finish this then," he said.

I pushed past the crowd, as faces flashed in a streaming blur. We entered a dark corridor lit only by black lights, which led into a large open space with a huge dance floor and an oval bar at its center. Colored lights glittered around the entire room. Strobe lights flickered on the dance floor from an elaborate lighting system tucked into the ceiling. The colored lights twirled in circles and bounced off the walls, throbbing to the bass-heavy techno music.

The strobe lights flickered giving us the appearance

of slow motion as we rushed through the crowded dance floor. The thumping music drowned out the explosions and gunfire from the parking lot, but as soon as security inside the club noticed our rifles they unleashed a barrage of bullets that cut through the air and fleeing customers became bloody collateral damage. I dove for cover behind a group of red leather booths that ran along a far wall. Bullets thudded into the leather cushions around me, but I stayed low waiting for the volley to end. As the shooters paused to reload I seized my opportunity, bolted up and returned fire taking out two members of the security squad. The wounds flowered through their clothes like red blossoms and they collapsed to the floor motionless.

The ruckus unexpectedly stopped when the music came to a screeching halt and the house lights came up, bright and sobering. This killed the murky nightclub mystique and the glaring floodlights blinded me for a few seconds until my eyes adjusted on a mortally tragic scene.

On the other side of the dance floor Danny knelt

wounded, held at gunpoint by Terry and Paul Gallagher. His face gaunt with a blood soaked jacket that indicated the severity of his injuries. Danny's head hung down on his chest in anguish and defeat while he awaited his ultimate fate. A familiar vile voice broke the solemn silence and spewed from speakers around the nightclub.

"Checkmate, motherfucker. Put down your weapon and get on the fuckin' floor," Vlad hissed.

I hesitated and searched for Vlad, but he was well hidden. I tried to size up a shot at the Gallaghers, but I didn't have a clear line of sight without hitting Danny.

"Shoot him!" Vlad demanded.

His voice vibrated over the nightclub speakers and I clenched my jaw in frustration at the thought of surrender. Paul Gallagher grinned, pressed the rifle barrel into Danny's head and he let out a grunt of distress.

"Okay, okay, hold it!" I screamed and dropped the rifle like it was red hot.

It clattered at my feet and slowly I lay down on my

belly with hands straight out, palms down and my eyes locked on the Gallaghers.

Terry Gallagher strutted across the dance floor with a swagger of confidence and pressed his pistol hard into the side of my head.

"Say goodbye, you cheeky prick," Terry said, with a sinister chuckle and cocked the mechanism back chambering a round.

I gritted my teeth and squeezed my eyes tight in anticipation when a sudden sound came out of nowhere. Two-foot steps cut through the air like a knife followed by a loud boom that echoed through the empty dance hall. Startled and surprised I looked up to see Doyle with a silver-plated .45 caliber automatic pistol in his hand. The top of Terry's head blew off as bits of brains, bone, and blood sprinkled down. Terry collapsed to his knees and onto his face as if someone had cut his puppet strings.

A loud horrible scream of agony and grief escaped Paul's mouth. The tip of his automatic rifle roared with fire as the floorboards around me erupted in splinters and sparks. Doyle got hit. He dropped his revolver as he went down. I grabbed his gun and crawled into the nearest booth, dragging Doyle under the table. I tried to fire back, but couldn't get a shot off.

Paul Gallagher seethed with rage his face locked in an evil grimace, his teeth bared and spittle oozing from his mouth. He stopped to reload his rifle, looking down to slam another magazine home. Danny rose from behind with his jacket full of blood and grabbed him in a tight bear hug. They collapsed onto the floor in an angry embrace.

Paul bucked and through his head back repeatedly. Danny's face became a bloody mess and he screamed an insane laugh and spit out a bloody tooth, but didn't let go. Blood streamed down his face in rivulets from gashes in his nose and forehead.

In a move that horrified and shocked me, Danny released the bear hug put both hands around Paul's head and snapped his neck. Paul's body thudded to the floor his head at a gruesome unnatural angle with eyes bulged and fixed on something far off spot in the distance.

Silence filled the nightclub, except for a slight pant from Danny. He sat on the floor, dazed, and wiped at the blood that ran down his face. I turned to check on Doyle and he crawled out from behind the booth with a wounded shoulder. He winced as he took out his mobile and called for help from the boys outside.

A rush of footsteps surprised me as a group of men ran out the back. The club backdoor slammed shut with a loud bang. I picked up Doyle's silver pistol and ran in pursuit.

I burst out the back door and into the frigid air, only to be peppered with bullets from an assault rifle. I dove for cover behind a large metal garbage container. A bald man I'd never seen before fired from the driver's window of a cargo truck.

Vlad held an Uzi on the passenger side of the truck and fired over the hood. I popped up and fired two shots that punctured the driver's door. Uninterested in the fight the driver yelled in Russian, shifted into gear and drove off. Vlad stumbled from the van and was left stunned, exposed and without cover. He retreated into the dark woods beyond the parking lot, slipped on an icy patch of snow and shot wildly into the sky. He recovered, ejected an empty magazine and reloaded. He ran deeper into the forest, ducked down, and disappeared behind a copse of trees that led to a basin.

I chased after him into the woods, my eyes slowly adjusted to the darkness and listened as Vlad made his way deeper into the forest and down towards the basin.

Snow crunched under my boots. I took a few steps and went still to listen for Vlad's footsteps. An eerie silence caught my attention and I froze hoping for a twig snap or the crunch of icy snow. Vlad's footsteps had also stopped and I peeked around a tree trunk eager to catch a glimpse, but couldn't see or hear him. I took a few deep breaths, listened to the wind howl and watched the steam puff from my mouth. I glanced up at the treetops, stared at the stars and tips of branches black against the dark blue night sky. I tried to remain calm and get a handle on the situation. A soft shuffling sound came from off in the distance, like an animal dragging something.

The sound led me to a steep incline of a frozen pond. Out in the middle of the frozen pond I could barely make out Vlad. I aimed carefully and squeezed the trigger. The sound echoed loudly and bounced through the trees. A crimson mist sprayed from Vlad's leg onto the snowy ice as the bullet passed through. He collapsed hard and crashed through the thin ice with a loud crack as if a mirror had shattered. He plunged into the bone-chilling water and struggled to grab hold of the edge, but couldn't. Desperately he fought to grab hold, but the pond continued to fracture and he couldn't stay a float. Vlad struggled to catch his breath, panted wildly with his eyes opened wide with terror. He shivered violently and grabbed at large floating chunks of ice, but was immediately dunked with each attempt.

"Give it up, Vlad, and I'll help you out."

"F-f-uck you!" He spat.

Vlad fired another barrage before the machine gun slipped out of his hand and he sank into the wintery slurry with a frantic gasp.

Seconds later he exploded to the surface, inhaled

heavily, gagged, and clawed at the edge of the broken ice. More chunks broke away the more he thrashed unable to find purchase. He gulped at the air and slipped under again. I watched with guilty satisfaction as Vlad became weaker and faded into the slushy water. The icy shattered pond became his tomb.

I stood in silence and watched for a few minutes. The last bubbles had stopped and I turned back towards the nightclub and listened to the echo of sirens as the Garda arrived a few hundred yards back.

I heard Chief Gerry's unmistakable voice over a megaphone.

"Give it up, boys. No one else has to die tonight. You're all done."

I looked back where Vlad had fallen through the ice and noticed a gray smoky shape drift out of the darkness. From behind a large dead tree a ghostly figure of a woman appeared, her gown clung tightly to her thin skeletal frame. Wisps of vapor trailed off her long hair and dress as she moved. She knelt down where Vlad had submerged, and let out an ear-piercing scream as she reached into the fractured hole and her image dissipated.

The hair on my neck stood on end followed and goose bumps rose all over my body. A chill ran up my spine and I rubbed at my eyes trying to decide if I was dreaming. I'd heard stories of Banshees stealing wounded warriors souls, but didn't believe it. A dizzy lightheadedness descended and the world did a stomach flipping turn.

Something warm and wet rolled down behind my ear. I thought it was sweat until I touched it and my hand came away red and slick with blood. One of Vlad's bullets had connected and a numb and nauseous feeling overtook me.

CHAPTER THIRTY-FIVE

I swallowed down hard and searched the sky for answers to explain what I'd just seen, but found none. I glanced at the treetops that swayed in the arctic wind and tried to remember what I was doing here and then sat up and glanced at the blood on my hand and the frozen basin.

I sluggishly hoisted myself up and trudged on in the opposite direction of the nightclub. I continued on for what felt like miles, until the sun rose and lit up the winter wonderland. Weak and frozen to the core I pushed on as tears streaked my face and immediately turned to ice. A bitter subzero wind gust stung my cheeks and the tips of my fingers and toes tingled with the beginnings of frostbite. After a while of slogging through this wintery wildness I was exhausted and could barely lift my legs anymore. I knelt on one knee, which instantly went cold, wet and numb. My time was running out. I peered through the trees and noticed a snowy path. I grabbed desperately at the tree branches for support, my hands frozen and raw as I pulled myself forward until I reached a road. Packed down with a messy mix of dirt and snow, the road led to an old farmhouse.

I staggered on. My feet and hands were now completely frozen. Urgently I attempted breath hot air on my fingertips to warm them, but it was no use. I cupped my burning ears to block the wind and felt icy blood that had crusted over and dragged myself closer to the farmhouse.

I followed the road as it curved down towards the shore and finally arrived at an old stonewall that defined the edge of the property. The old farmhouse stood as a solitary black silhouette on the horizon. The night continued to recede, replaced by a fiery red and orange daybreak. Large snowdrifts blocked a clear path to the house. It appeared unkempt and deserted, but I struggling on. I'm not sure how much blood I'd lost, but I leaned on the wall spent as another wave of weakness racked my body.

I approached the front of the farmhouse small

brown birds chattered and flitted about. The bird's tucked their heads down in their fluffy feathers to evade the cold. A few fluttered away from my heavy steps, while others watched and waited in the bare bushes that lined the front yard. I dragged myself onto the porch on trembling legs that barely worked and realized someone lived here. The snow had been swept away, and a pile of seeds was left for the birds. A broom sat against the wall next to a set of old chairs that had been dusted clean. I groped at a wooden railing and pulled myself up a short set of stairs and onto the porch.

My vision blurred and filled with dark spots at the edges. I collapsed face first onto the wooded porch, snow and seeds scattered in my wake.

I awoke in bed, dazed and sore. Warmth engulfed my entire body and a pleasant familiar aroma of home cooking filled my senses. I glanced at the heavy blankets that cover me and examined my surroundings. I lay in an unfinished room framed in wood like a hunting cabin. Light came through a single frozen window coated with ice and I could hear people talking in another room, but couldn't make out their exact words. I soon realized it was a woman humming a soft melody. I sat up and the blankets slid off my shoulders. I knew this was a bad idea when my head swooned with a spell of dizziness that made me shudder. The top of my ears felt hot and tight and I reached up and felt gauze wrapped around my head. No sign of the crusty wound I'd suffered earlier.

A plump old woman with silver hair in a ponytail and glasses entered the room. She wore a floral dress and shuffled in with a tray of roasted lamb, vegetables, bread, and tea. She hummed unaware of my eyes on her and placed a tray on the table next to the bed.

"Well, hello there. You're up? How are you feeling?"

Gently she propped the pillows and pulled the blankets to my shoulders.

"Better, but dizzy," I said.

"That's a good sign. You've taken quiet a nasty gash to your head, son. I did my best, but a doctor should tend to that." She adjusted her glasses on her nose.

I reached under the blanket for my phone only to

find I had no pants. A little rattled, I nervously searched the room and found my clothes cleaned and folded neatly on a chair at the foot of the bed.

"I'm Sarah. What's your name, son?" she asked, with a pleasant smile.

"I'm Bill. Did you happen to find a phone?"

I tried to get out of bed, but winced as a sharp spike of pain shot through my head.

"Oh, you shouldn't go anywhere yet, you poor dear."

"I'm not, I just need to call someone."

"Of course," she said. She handed me my phone then left the room.

I pressed the buttons desperate to call Janette, but it was dead. The phone had been my last hope to get out of here quickly. I dropped it on the bed and sighed in exasperation.

Sarah came shuffling back in the room after hearing my frustration.

"What is it dear?"

"I need to get back to my girl in Dublin. She's probably a nervous wreck without knowing I'm safe."

Outside I heard the loud roar of a truck engine. Startled I jumped out of bed and quickly got dress, my head ached, but I pushed the pain down. I tried to look outside, but the window was covered with ice except for a small patch. A large black 4x4 pickup truck with a snowplow cleared a path from the road to the farmhouse.

"Don't be alarmed, Bill. That's just me son, Jamie. He's come to clean up a bit after the snow storm."

I felt extremely vulnerable and realize I didn't have Doyle's silver gun. Panic overwhelmed me and Sarah watched my face as I anxiously searched the room and drawers of a nearby cabinet.

"Did you find anything else in my clothes or jacket?" I asked.

"No dear, I didn't."

"I had something very important I can't find."

"Settle down, Jamie can take you into Dublin when he's finished."

I'd been so out of sorts that I didn't know what to do. I grabbed my jacket off the back of the chair and immediately felt the weight of the pistol in the pocket.

"Where are you rushing too? Don't you want Jamie to help you?" she asked, a concerned expression on her face.

"I'm sorry, I don't feel myself," I said.

"Of course dear, you're still weak from that gash."

Relief spilled over my exhausted body. I sat down on the bed and place my jacket besides me. I squeeze my jacket pocket, felt the shape of the gun and relaxed a little more.

"Here, have something to eat and you'll feel better." Sarah handed me the plate of food from the tray. The roast tasted unbelievable, soft pieces of lamb with vegetables that immediately warmed my stomach. I took a chunk of bread from the tray and dipped it into the gravy, then scooped it right into my mouth. I had no idea how long I'd been without food, but this meal was incredibly delicious. I shoveled it into my mouth and cleaned the plate with the last piece of bread. I wiped my mouth with my hand and found a beard. How many days had I been here? It felt like a week's worth of growth.

My stomach full, I became groggy and fell into a

deep food-induced coma.

"Hey, mate." A male voice woke me from my nap. He leaned over and violently shook my shoulder.

"C'mon, wake up. What are you doing here?" he asked.

"Okay, hold on. Take it easy," I said, and sat up.

A ginger-haired man in his thirties with a straggly beard pointed Doyle's silver .45 at my face. He wore a black turtleneck sweater and blue jeans with tan work boots.

"I don't know what you're about, but get out of me Mum's house, now," he growled.

"Sorry, a branch hit me and I was freezing to death when your Mom took me in."

"I don't care about your fuckin' troubles. Now get out before I forget me Mum's gentle ways and shoot you in your eye."

He motioned me out with the gun and we both stood up slowly. Jamie was taller than I expected and he took a couple of steps back. I reached for my jacket and turned. He seemed nervous, but did a great job staying out of my reach with Doyle's gun focused on me.

I gave the performance of my career and fainted, collapsing like a sack of potatoes off the side of the bed and fell hard onto the floor with a gasp.

"Oh Jesus. Are your fuckin' kiddin' me?" He blurted, in disgust.

Jamie nudged me with his boot, but my unresponsiveness encouraged him to put the gun into his waistband. He bent down to pick up my apparently unconscious body. I continued my hoax and hung dead and lifeless until he had both hands wrapped around me. I grabbed the gun from his waistband and pressed it against his freckled nose.

"Move and I'll add another hole to your skull. Now back off and give me your keys. I'm gonna take your ride," I snarled.

Jamie took out his keys and placed them in my outstretched palm. I pressed the gun harder into his face to make sure he didn't try anything stupid. I pulled the gun away, which left an angry red indent and let out a big breath. His eyes followed the gun and I was sure I had his full attention.

"I'll take your phone too," I demanded.

He handed over a gray flip phone and I opened it to check that it worked.

"Get in there and act like we're old pals. Your mom's been kind to me and I don't want to upset her. Now move," I ordered.

Jamie led the way into the living room with my gun at his back. I shoved it hard into his spine and shoved him along.

"Smile and tell her we have to go into town." I whispered.

"Umm… Hey, Mum, I'm gonna run your friend into town so he can head home," Jamie said.

"Thank you, Sarah, for your hospitality. You have excellent nursing skills," I teased.

"Oh stop it. You better get yourself to a doctor."

I pushed Jamie out the front door and off the porch. I motioned him to get in the truck.

"You're driving and don't think I won't pull this trigger. Don't be a trickster and you'll be home in time for lunch with your lovely mum."

I climbed into the driver's side and slid over with

the gun pointed at his chest. The truck roared to life and we bounced through the snow towards the city. After twenty minutes we hit the outskirts of Dublin and I had Jamie pull to the shoulder.

"What now?" he asked, with a concerned expression.

"You get out and walk. Keep walking and you'll find your truck a few miles up the road," I said.

"No, you can't take my truck."

"Look, I don't want to hurt you, but I'll give you three seconds to get out. One, two, three."

Jamie lunged for the gun, but I dodged his attempt and hit him with the butt. His head rocked back and he instantly held his face as blood ran out from between his fingers. Jamie's eyes rolled back in his head and he fought to keep conscious, but I opened the driver's door and kicked him out. I slid into the driver's seat, peeked out to see if he was okay and pulled away.

CHAPTER THIRTY-SIX

It was freezing cold out. The temperature had dropped drastically and a bitter December squall was creeping into my bones. It had to be below zero and the wind-chill made it feel even colder. My breath puffed steam like an engine, which hung in the fridge air before dissipating into the night.

I stayed in the shadows, hugging myself and occasionally stamping my feet for warmth. A shiver ran up my spine and I shook it off with a grunt. I turned up my collar and watched as an indistinguishable figure came out the back and stood in the open doorway. The light from behind created a crisp black silhouette and cast a long shadow that rolled down the stairs. He pulled out a lighter, flipped it open, and lit a thick cigar. It glowed brightly in the darkness and he cupped the flame against the wind. His face appeared with each puff as the flames flared, I was sure this was my man.

He came down the stairs with weighed steps and smoke bellowed around him as if his head was a cinder. His keys jingled as he opened the car door and sat down.

I moved noiselessly towards him slowly at first and then sped up. My boots tapped at the ground in an odd rhythm that built to an accelerated pace. I approached his open car door and peered in where he sat. He looked up and reached inside his jacket, but his old reflexes were too slow. The silencer made one hiss as the bullet penetrated his forehead.

Chief Gerry crumpled out of his car and onto the black pavement in a lifeless heap. The cigar fell from his mouth, bounced with a burst of sparks and rolled out of sight. The car door illuminated his face, with eyes bulged wide as if in his final moment something had horrified him in the night sky. The Chief's greed had led him to this crossroad and he got his just desserts. His soul if he had one was headed to a new resting place.

Blood poured out from the exit wound like black oil and pooled on the asphalt. Dark and shiny, it reflected my movements as I stepped over his body and rushed to a waiting car. The driver put it in gear and pressed the accelerator hard. We pulled away from the curb the rear tires smoked and kicked up gravel as we raced away.

No one had topped a police chief on Irish soil in a long time and there'd be a lot of heat on Doyle's operations, but I really didn't care. I wasn't sticking around anyway.

ABOUT THE AUTHOR

Garrard Hayes is a lifelong New York resident whose ancestors made their living on the streets of Manhattan and Brooklyn. His love of action and crime fiction, together with a knack for good, gritty storytelling, sparked him to write. He lives in New York with his wife, two children, and three dogs. Please follow him on Twitter @garrardhayes or visit garrardhayes.com for his book review blog and more information about his writing.

www.ingramcontent.com/pod-product-compliance
Lightning Source LLC
Chambersburg PA
CBHW031212120726

47905CB00002B/303